ISBN 978-1-331-24391-5
PIBN 10163496

1 MONTH OF
FREE
READING

at

www.ForgottenBooks.com

By purchasing this book you are eligible for one month membership to ForgottenBooks.com, giving you unlimited access to our entire collection of over 700,000 titles via our web site and mobile apps.

To claim your free month visit:

www.forgottenbooks.com/free163496

English
Français
Deutsche
Italiano
Español
Português

www.forgottenbooks.com

Mythology Photography **Fiction** Fishing Christianity **Art** Cooking Essays Buddhism Freemasonry Medicine **Biology** Music **Ancient Egypt** Evolution Carpentry Physics Dance Geology **Mathematics** Fitness Shakespeare **Folklore** Yoga Marketing **Confidence** Immortality Biographies Poetry **Psychology** Witchcraft Electronics Chemistry History **Law** Accounting **Philosophy** Anthropology Alchemy Drama Quantum Mechanics Atheism Sexual Health **Ancient History** **Entrepreneurship** Languages Sport Paleontology Needlework Islam **Metaphysics** Investment Archaeology Parenting Statistics Criminology **Motivational**

ITTLE PEOPLE

BY

ARD WHITEING

A *The Island," " No. 5, John Street," " All Moonshine,"*

LIMITED

NEW YORK, TORONTO & MELBOURNE

MCMVIII

LITTLE PEOPLE

BY

RICHARD WHITEING

Author of " The Island," " No. 5, John Street," " All Moonshine,"
etc. etc.

CASSELL & COMPANY, LIMITED
London, Paris, New York, Toronto & Melbourne
MCMVIII

CONTENTS

LITTLE PEOPLE

THE FAMILY LIKENESS

THE Irish have a beautiful fancy, but you must know them and they must know you before they will make you free of it. So qualified, you will learn, in the strictest confidence, that you have only to rise at dawn to see the Little People going home. They have been out all night on business, and now they are running back to their subterranean abodes. The Little People are the ancient inhabitants of the country, still waiting for a turn of the luck, and meanwhile lying low. They take the air under the starlight, with other creatures that have scant fellowship with man, but the first streak of day drives them in a twinkling to the burrows or the clefts of the rocks.

It has often struck me that this is an apologue as well as a myth. What are the Little People but a section of the quiet folk who form the vast majority of our kind? You may count the race of man by any other categories of politics, literature, science, or art, but these severally are as nothing to the mighty preponderance of Little

B

Peopledom among those who just want to keep themselves to themselves and who have no relish for the coarser excitements of life. Their name is Legion of Legion, for they cross and interfuse all the others, and they form a multitude which is the lowest common denominator. If you could have them for the census it would be almost unnecessary to tabulate the rest. You may be a peer and a Little Person, or you may be a peasant, a duchess or a needlewoman: Little Peopledom alone counts in the last resort.

It is like Freemasonry in its kind of power, while far exceeding it in the degree. A Lord Mayor on the Bench was once driven to remark with some severity that he could take no notice of the sign when it came from brother Masons in the dock. This irregularity, of course, was no impeachment of the morals of the Order at large. It meant no more than that, when Freemasonry happened to include the sinner as well as the saint, the sinner should play fair. Now Little Peopledom has a still wider embrace: it is only less of a general characteristic than the nose on your face, and only less variously inclusive than the order of the mammalia.

To describe it by some of its negations, it may be defined as an order of fellow creatures who rarely get into the papers. The interviewers know it not, the special commissioners pass it by. It is " you and I," for the vast majority of those concerned in our present survey. It is in one of its sections, but only one, the losers in the game of life—the cricketers who are usually put out with the first ball, the candidates at examinations who take the duck's egg, the vast mass of worthy and often quite lovable people who can't make a do of it and who are quite content to take the consequences.

Sitting snugly in my place in the omnibus, and hearing the conductor's fateful cry of " Room for one ! " at the first halting-place, I know that a Little Peopler will never be that one, unless he happens to be the only applicant for a seat. And, even then, he is sure to be dispossessed by his own volition at the next stage should a lady—or, as he might call her, a female—hail the vehicle before it has gone a dozen yards. He may be exactly like everybody else in outward seeming, but concealed somewhere about his spiritual personality there is sure to be the badge of his vocation. He is one of those who don't want to fight, not necessarily that he lacks nerve and sinew for the encounter, but mainly because he feels that his victory means another's defeat. Sometimes, of course, he is a mere " duffer," but here again a subtler diagnosis would still reveal the soft spot of pity for those weaker than himself and a quite abnormally developed readiness to oblige.

Women by myriads are in this vast array, with all others who can neither enter the lists in their own persons nor find a champion. To be fair, these discomfited ones sometimes move the compassion of their conquerors. When the fight is over—though naturally not in the course of it—a generous winner will not disdain to cast an eye on the fallen, and even to offer them a word of consolation on his way to reap the fruits of victory.

Dear to me are these Quietists high and low. They are all alike in this : they want to keep themselves to themselves, to narrow the circle of their interests by making it conterminous with that of their friendships and their loves. Yet they must still have it large enough to include some hobby that is without a taint of self-seeking, some favourite study at need. I have known some go so far as to plead for a favourite weakness, and I can meet them cheerfully on that ground, and compare notes in fads.

An heir to a peerage, of my acquaintance, got himself formally enrolled as a Little Peopler by the simple process of bolting from a noble circle and leaving no address. They sought him high and low, advertised for him, sent his portrait to the police to figure among notices of runaway husbands or stray donkeys in the pound—to be sold to pay expenses if not claimed within ten days. Meanwhile he was quietly engaged as a common seaman before the mast, in immeasurable voyages round the Horn, or what not, with no events but the alternations of sunshine and storm, and vigils under the stars. He was a mere hand in the fo'c'sle, with his quality for his own secret, and with a label of Jack or Jem for identification by his mates.

For years he lay thus in successful hiding from the House of Lords, from dinner party and from house party, from the meet and the charity chairmanship, from all the futilities of patronage and of social leadership. He loved his quid and his yarn, his " Yo ho! heave ho! " at the ropes, his clean shirt and clean dick for the Sabbath day. And he gave us all the slip to the last. For his secret never came out till he lay dying, and he timed his reckoning so nicely for this proceeding that they were obliged to give him his sepulture in mid-ocean, while the ancestral vault yawned for him in vain. I have never heard that he made any last dying speech and confession of a misspent life.

On the contrary, there is every reason to believe that he called for his pipe and he called for his glass as long as he was able to relish these delicacies, and went out to the slow music of the fo'c'sle fiddle with the missing string. He had had his good time of peace and quietness, and the commerce of simple souls of his own spiritual order, and he was quite ready to depart, with the hope, no doubt, of sublimated joys of the same sort in another sphere.

Now this man was but one of the annual lists

of the lost that are so strangely misread if we construe them solely as runaway bankrupts, defaulting cashiers, fathers of families with quivers over-full, or ratepayers in elopement with members of the *corps de ballet*. Many of them are simply Molinists on the run from the hurly-burly, and perhaps from the haunting fear of having to yield. to really evil temptations in a too fatuous pursuit of the joy of life.

I knew of another man, as we all knew of him till the hue and cry dropped, who fled from pulpit and rectory into the void, until he was found urging cattle to market and in a drover's smock. His bold venture for freedom had miscarried. They stopped him and claimed him—in whose name no human being, themselves included, could fairly understand—and led him back into the slavery of his family circle. His life was quite inglorious thereafter, and he was never heard of again. One may plausibly imagine him passing the rest of it in the irons of a social position altogether foreign to his tastes, his smock exchanged for the comfortless uniform of his order, his belcher for the white choker which was but the old collar of medieval serfage with a gentler clasp.

The biggest of all the Little People was Spinoza, who wrought out the noblest of all speculations in philosophy and religion in the intervals of his work as an artisan. I like to think of this truly fine figure of a man, in the setting of his workshop, quite as much as in the setting of his study. Perhaps the two were one. At any rate there was the daily toil for the modest tribute due to Cæsar, and then the nightly service of the universal Being whose infinite attributes he yet managed to define. He must remain the highest expression of the scholar-workman for all time.

In every age select souls like his have laboured for Saturday night's wages and for the redemption of the world. Sometimes they have drudged in meaner toil, and for a mere payment, in kind, of provender. I am not forgetful of Epictetus in the slave lairs of Rome. It is an enduring type, and we have but to use our eyes to find it in a particularly beautiful efflorescence in our societies of to-day.

The student is not always so happy in his craft as the polisher of lenses. A little too often for his liking, though he makes the best of it, he is in the busy haunts of men as bread-winner, selling over the counter, driving a quill in the giant clearing houses, tramping the streets on commission. But the night cometh for the lecture-room and the class-room, and for what follows when the highest set forth to visit him across the continents and across the ages, in a garret that is also a grove of Academe. I have caught him here, kneeling at his books for fear of sleeping over them if he kept his chair, and now and again stretched full length on the floor in the utter darkness of an

exhausted lamp, and waking at my touch to wonder if he is still a denizen of the world. Happy
the great Jew with nothing discordant between his
daily tale of service for a living and his nightly
excursions into the empyrean of thought.

All these are the happy Little People who are
amorous of the quiet life. The permanent clerks
in the Government offices, the silent, capable men
who carry all India or all England in their brain,
and who keep the peace while their prancing
scholars take the floor of the House, are often
of the secret guild of this companionship. Little
People, Little People, every mother's son of them;
all honour to the breed! But this would be fanei-
ful, and we must not go too far. These last are
the Little People only in being the quiet people,
people of the still water that runs deep. And, as
they are so often persons of the first importance,
there may be a certain shock to the mind in having
them included at all. Perhaps I include them for
that reason, for the sake of the shock of paradox,
and just to emphasise the fact that the unobtrusive
people are not by any means to be confounded
with the unimportant.

Yet, after all, as they do sometimes catch the
limelight in a momentary flash, they are hardly
suited to my great subject, the people that are of
no account in the world's esteem. I have known
what it is to find these still, strong people of the
departments in a Birthday List, with a K.C.B. as

a handle to their name. I think they are usually belittled by such notice, but this is by the way. My great, my abiding, my predominant theme is the gentle or simple, the heroes, or the other thing, who never " get a hand." Could I make it so, this should be the prose Iliad of that folk. To achieve this, however, would be to deliver them to publicity, and so to defeat my own end. I want to be moderate and reasonable, and to avoid the pitfall. The true Little People, and the dear, the vast central body of the host, as distinguished from the skirmishers and the wings, are the average people, many of them failures as we reckon success, some of them incompetent, all of no account. Here we are on firm ground, for we are with the vast majority of all nations, of all mankind.

It is something pathetic to see how many of them there are. Take a walk in town, and they flit by you in their forties of thousands, all flitting like one—little men, little women, little children especially, and all bearing the mark of their vocation. Yet each one, like the midges in a swarm, is a life, a life with organs, a heart, for instance, that might be detected under the microscope, nerves that know how to quiver with pain under the skilful application of a pin's point, and withal, every other spring and cog of the machinery that keeps the world on the go. The little men are chiefly commerce and our empire of trade, the little women, not infrequently, the vestalhood of the Postal Service or of the copyist craft; the little children too often, in their neglected condition, the potentiality of failure and crime.

These last, I think, are the most pathetic figures. The thought struck me the other day, when I was scouring a gloomy district in Bow under the guidance of the head mistress of a Board School. It was her weekly visit to the parents of her charges in the infant department, with whom she had to make interest—just as the heads of the more fashionable establishments of this kind make interest with the elect of the Red Book—for the benefit of all concerned. The casual labourers and their wives had to be placated, or the children might not be sent to school at all. Her pupils ran out to meet her as she went from one dwarf dwelling to another, and clung to her skirts or clasped her hand.

It was Saturday, and therefore play-day, and many of them were in undress. One young gentleman (potential), to be quite frank about it, went too far in this direction. He was scarcely— perhaps he had not expected company : well, he wore nothing in the world but a paternal waist-coat, that, while fairly, and as I thought fortun-ately, engulfing the whole upper part of his person, left all the rest completely bare. He crawled about in it, like a small tortoise in the shell of a turtle which had parted its garments in preparation for a civic feast. But this is only by the way. He was chubby, cheerful, and unwashed for the holiday. He was especially most affectionate, and he offered a cheek to his teacher, whereon, with marvellous deftness—bred, no doubt, of long practice—she picked a least unsuitable spot for the *accolade*.

I asked her as to his proficiency in humane letters, and she assured me that he stood well in his class, and that many of the others left little to be desired in that respect. They were bright, intelligent, eager, curious—everything that children at that age should be—keen for the object lessons, quick and inventive in all, and generally wanting nothing but the chance to grow up into little angels in Eton suits. I congratulated her, but could not forbear the remark that it must be a pang to her to prepare them in this way for perfect manhood and womanhood, only to have them at last handed over to destiny for the Little Peopledom of the slums. Imagine the feeling of the potter when the bull gets loose in the china shop. All this labour, all this care, all this beauty of result; and then for a subsequent field of action the dock gates, the pawnbroker's, the corner pin, and generally the London mud, in both kinds, as the only soil for their bedding out.

" There is our tragedy," she said.

THE RATEPAYER

THE main body of the Little People, as distinguished from the wings and fringes, is the host of the Ratepayers. They are to be seen at their best only in England, the paradise of local taxation. This new label, which I humbly offer, indicates not merely a civic status, but a frame of mind, a true inward consciousness of vocation far transcending the responsibilities of quarter day. There is a ratepayer spirit, a ratepayer soul; the world abounds in ratepayers who are quite unknown to the lists at the church doors. They are the aspirants, the novices of the order, and, in due course, they will give such proofs of their calling as will entitle them to a place on the register.

For that matter, the actual payment of rates is of quite secondary importance. What truly counts is the inward and spiritual grace, that sees in the mere function certain finite ends of being whereof respectability is the first. I have known genuine ratepayers of the tenderest years—all schoolmasters will bear me out—I have met others who have failed to qualify in the spiritual way at threescore and ten. This would be my reply to the rash assertion that, as mere persons with a roof of our own over our heads, we are all ratepayers. Nothing of the sort. We have had a remarkable book on the soul of a people : my greater theme is the soul of a parishioner.

This was brought home to me once by a little adventure I met with in one of my walks. I had strayed into a garden adjoining a public recreation ground, a garden with an open gate. I thought that the two enclosures were one for the purposes of public use. I had advanced, however, but a very little way, when a huge dog came running towards me and sounding the alarm. He was followed by a woman, who emerged from a sort of lodge, and who met my gaze of inquiry by a look of displeasure. " What's your business, please ? " It might have been more considerately put, but the significance was clear enough—I was a trespasser.

There is perhaps no more embarrassing position for one brought up in a land rooted in the idea of property. Other irregularities admit of some defence—passion, feeling, the sense of a mission, or what not—for this there is none. Invincible ignorance may, of course, serve in a way, but this still exposes you to the humiliation of being told that it is your business to know. I should have done well, no doubt, to choose it, and to bear the consequences; yet I must avow with shame that I could not bear the thought of having to lower myself in the woman's eyes. She herself looked so thoroughly respectable that I wished her to respect me; and so, in the perturbation of my spirits, I fell into a meanness. I sought to win her regard by a manœuvre which was really nothing to the point. For I waived the direct charge of trespass, and fell back on the wholly irrelevant plea of my station in society.

"It is hard," I said, "that a ratepayer cannot walk through an open gate." It was magical in its effect. Her whole manner changed in a moment; she cuffed the dog with her apron, the severity went out of her regard, and she forthwith began to stammer an apology. The tables were turned, and I took base advantage of the situation by forgiving her on the spot. With that I turned to leave, but she would not have it so. "I beg your pardon, sir; it was my little girl's fault in leaving the gate open when she went to school. Take a look round, and welcome as the flowers in May." We were friends now, and she did the honours of the enclosure with an air of repentance that touched me to the quick.

This was a turning point in my life. I saw that I had stumbled on a new classification of humanity, and that I might go down to posterity as a Cuvier of the higher plane. A ratepayer for more years than I cared to count, I had for the first time realised the majesty of my part. It was no longer a mere condition : it was a point of view, a way of looking at life.

I now saw that there was a ratepayer spirit in the highest affairs: in politics and in patriotism, in poetry, nay, religion itself. To define it by one of its opposites, it was everything that was not Quixotic; the hero of Cervantes, in his final scene —the significance of which has been so strangely missed—not only repenting of his heroism, but realising himself as primarily a householder with all that the obligation imports.

The ratepayer is, in fact, the great general type dominating all others, and knowing no variation but that of its name in all lands. In France this standardised fellow creature is known as Monsieur Jourdain, or as Monsieur Prudhomme—the latter for my choice; in Germany he has the dual personality of Schülz and Müller. In Switzerland he bears a hundred names, most of them names of hotel-keepers. In him the bold, indomitable mountaineers of the heresies and the insurrections have come to a compromise with all the reactions.

After giving to the world a Calvin and a Rousseau, not to speak of the Swiss infantry and the guard that died for Louis XVI., they have very contentedly settled down into a community of inn-keepers, with waiters for their chief article of export—a nation of ratepayers, in a word. Their President is now the representative man of their new outlook on life. Whatever else he may not be, he is bound to be obscure—a general practitioner, by preference, pilling and blistering in the intervals of the business of state—and a very Dalai Lama in the absolute ignorance of so much as his name on the part of the majority of mankind.

But for an accident, the great Napoleon himself would have been a ratepayer and the head of the order. For has not de Bourrienne, the chronicler of his youth of poverty and neglect, told us of their joint project of starting a boarding-house? Most precious, this, of all the fragments of biography, for, with it, we come to the highest and the broadest reaches of the science of the might-have-been. They failed only, I believe, for want of funds, in a day when the hire system was unknown. But if they had not failed? Imagine the sallow youth with the Imperial profile and the eagle eye, at the head of a dining-room table instead of a council board, and catering small talk and resurrection pie for Père Goriot and the rest in a *pension* of the fourth class. Implicit in him, but never to be unfolded, would have been the eloquence of the bulletins, and the dread brevities of the crisis of battle, with banded nations moving as one to do his will.

Think of a genius of captaincy that taught Cæsar and Hannibal to know their place putting down a riot in a drawing-room for the seat nearest the fire!—of a genius of Italian statecraft that reduced Machiavelli to the rank of a course for beginners diplomatising to change Madame

Bobinot from the bedroom with the cretonne hangings to the bedroom with the rep, on the persuasion that it will be better for her cold. And think again of the universal provider, who fed the French Army on its marches, huckstering in all the markets of his quarter to save another sou in the franc on the dinner of the day!

It was a freak of Providence that took him into the other sphere. Why not have left him alone? With such a Protector for our order, we might have cried " Wha daur meddle wi' me ? " to a world in arms. Perhaps he was with us after all. He might have been a saviour of the revolution : he elected to be an Emperor of the Ratepayers. The best of rulers are but servants of servants— ourselves in the highest; but when they happen to be ourselves in the lowest, Heaven help!

It is the same with all lordship whatsoever; the tribal deities, and not merely those in the South Seas, are ratepayers to a man. And I know of far more elaborate theological systems wherein our order gets more than its share. They are so hard on the stupid and incompetent, so full of loving-kindness towards the smugly prosperous, so long-suffering with the faults of wealth and station, while visiting the slightest peccadillo of the lowly with the torments of the pit.

With a more even-handed system the rate-payer ought to find more stones in his path of redemption. Just when he is settling down to the

c

rewards of a misspent life, the sins of his youth should crowd in on him like so many summonses for debt. They should demand a settlement, not only with the threat of social exposure, but sometimes in the much more serious form of their effect on his moral nature. The crooked in him would have to be made straight, at the cost of agonising wrenches to his entire system.

Mighty is the ratepayer, and, do what you may, he will have his rights. As I passed a great restaurant the other day there was the usual hurly-burly of people going in to guzzle, with cab and carriage and motor discharging their loads at the portal. What a difference, I thought, between this hunger for the feast of the body, and the hunger for the feast of the soul as you find it perhaps in next door's meeting-house, with nothing but religion or philosophy for the fare. Sainthood at one end of the scale, so often with a beggarly account of empty boxes; at the other, the triumphant ratepayer, like youth, determined to be served.

CHILDHOOD

I THINK little people generally begin as the very biggest people : I mean that childhood is the age of the greatest keenness and freshness of intuitions in both kinds, white and black. We start as heroes, whether of the asphodel or of the burning marl; and, in this part of our being, grow downwards into ratepayers, quite reversing the mere physical process of altitude and cubic content. The ratepayer was once a child, with a sense of life as a scene of good endeavour in chivalry, all compact. I am often favoured by the confidences of one of that species, and he tells me, with a sort of shame, that nothing can exceed the silliness of the fancies that used to trot through his head— before he knew the world. He means before he forgot the other world; but why not let him tell his own tale in his own way ?

He had, it seems, a rooted idea that nothing succeeds, or at any rate ought naturally to succeed, like ill success. If you cannot get on, why, of course, people will press forward to help you. It would be impossible to keep them back. Their hearts would go out to you as the child's heart goes out to the lame dog, the winged bird; and you would be overwhelmed with ministrations.

You might have to put advertisements in the papers: "No more help wanted at No. 13." Therefore—"I was but a kid, you know," he always takes care to say—he never could make out why his tradesmen should be so foolishly anxious to proclaim the fact that they were doing better than their neighbours. A tuck shop rashly lost my friend's infant custom by announcing a surfeit of prosperity. This only led him to consider the case of the other shops starving for patronage, and to transfer his orders for jam puffs to an old lady in a back street. He may have been well advised or ill advised—he thought the latter was the case—but such was the effect.

Childhood is not usually the age of compromise or the second thought. It has all its colour impressions in primitives, and daubs the whole scene in red, blue, and yellow; yellow, blue, and red. It is commonly the age of generous enterprises, of knightly service for the oppressed, of pity for the vanquished, though these may have figured as oppressors in their turn—of all the Quixotisms, in a word. Even when it is something less than this, in its aggressiveness of high spirits it is still capable of all sorts of returns upon itself.

Full well did my ratepayer remember his first fight. It was a dormitory fight in nightgowns, the provocation having arisen at the morning hour. He had found an old boy of six months' standing ragging another who had arrived but the night before. It was a bad case, according to the ethics of the ward, a bad case for the new boy : he had been caught snivelling for his mammy on going to bed. Snivelling is not Spartan : he had been forthwith well belaboured with pillows as a sedative, and with the hope that he might wake next day in a manlier frame of mind. The feeling against the sufferer had been exacerbated by the failure of the prescription. His physicians had done their best for him, but, instead of working with them, he had been distinctly heard snivelling again during the night. His detector, and the principal adviser of the ward, was now about to repeat the dose, always for the good of the patient.

But here my ratepayer came in as one unable to see eye to eye with his colleagues, and, moved by a noble rage, he sprang from his own couch, and the battle began. The stars in their courses have a sneaking kindness for champions of this sort. At the end of the third round the senior physician's head struck the floor by the sheer accident of an awkward fall. The head was but slightly damaged as it afterwards turned out, but it emitted a sound so hollow that everyone, and particularly the owner, was struck with a sense of catastrophe, though it was really but an ordinary case of a misfit in brains. The bully was beaten, and there should have been an end of the matter.

But the victorious ratepayer yet to be would not leave it there. His heart smote him with pity for the foe, and he kissed the sore place, as, in like case, his own bruises had been kissed a hundred times. He could not help wondering how the dormitory would take it, but he was soon reassured. Forgetting itself in a momentary reversion to its childhood at the mother's knee, it roared with delight, and presented him with gifts, one of them a penknife in quite tolerable repair.

I dwell particularly on this case of reversion because I maintain that these finer movements of the spirit are natural to the child. They are within him—with their opposites, of course—ready to be drawn out by anybody who knows how to do it. The mother is one of those who best know; and it is a pity, I think, that the boy is withdrawn from her so soon. With the finer instincts, no doubt, are also the coarser ones, since the battle has to be refought everlastingly in each individual soul, and it takes two to make a fight. Individually the dormitory had begun as well as anybody, but left to itself too soon, without the finer guidance, its better part had not had fair play. All dormitories are like that, for the simple reason that scholarly males are not the best dry nurses for infant souls. In the case under consideration, perhaps, the mother had been longer in charge.

But, there, who can tell?—and it is really quite immaterial. It is enough that the finer instincts which were in all of them—as witness the burst of jubilation and the gifts—had, in this case by a happy accident, suffered no rebirth into barbarism. The others had to recover their tone: this ratepayer's had not been lost. The premature loss of it, by the process known as hardening the boyish nature, is one of the most regrettable things in school life. It always comes about a dozen years too soon, not to say a hundred, for, truth to tell, it need never come at all. The brave things are things that are beautiful as well, and it seems a pity to get rid of them prematurely by a sort of surgical operation in fagging. The boy is, so to speak, inoculated with the disease of fierceness in his tenderest years, and there ought to be more scope in this matter for the conscientious objector.

It is a great shock when a youngster, who has had to be dragged from a woman's neck to enable him to leave home for the first time, returns to it in a few short months unwilling to meet any one of that sex in an embrace, for fear of *lèse majesté* to his manhood. "Must we kiss them?" whispered a dot of this kind on attending a tea party to meet the small sisters of a friend. A few years hence, and what might he not be willing to give for the privilege; but let us not anticipate.

To my mind the really striking thing about children is their passion for getting at the truth. They have come into a strange planet—from what other we do not know—and they naturally want to master its laws. They are as we all should be on entering a new community; the first thing asked for would be a copy of the rules and regulations. They want the facts. This goes far beyond a passion for the mere yea and nay of ordinary communication. They have rich reserves of both good and bad in them, and they must know on which they are to draw, and who is master in their new world, the spirit of their finer intuitions, or the spirit of the others. Whatever answer is given to them, they will take it for the literal truth they are longing for, and their respect for such truth will make them the whole-hoggers of either event.

Breed them in an environment of lying, knavery, violence as the law of being, and they will follow these things out of their very respect for truth. It is such a world: then so be it, though the inner voice may whisper its protest unheard. But this sort of protest is rather the infirmity of second childhood. Grown people, even the worst, learn to lack conviction in their wickedness; badly brought up children have none—they have put all their energy of confidence into the career. The orders and brotherhoods of crime, the banded gangs of robbery or murder sometimes found in the depths, invariably have extreme youth as their note. Their oaths and their passwords bespeak the sentiment of a vocation, the homage to a law. Give them the right law (and you can only do it by working on their sense of artistry), and they will be quite ready to associate as children of light. " Under which king, Bezonian ? " They want the facts about their fealties, first and last and all the time.

This hunt for the truth, good or bad, coupled with their natural confidence in their elders, makes very young people ready to believe everything they are told. It is quite awful to think how absolutely, how accusingly they take us at our word. The real turning point in a child's life is not so much the first lie he tells as the first he finds out—a lie on the side of virtue or a lie on the side of vice; it is all one in its effects. The story of the infant Washington might more profitably be transposed, with the father coming to confession before the child.

My brother ratepayer used to assure me that, in the earlier stage of his earthly pilgrimage, he had absolutely no idea of speech as a means for the concealment of thought. Inquiring, in due course of his tenderest years, as to the methods of catching birds, he was told, again in due course, that he had nothing to do but put a pinch of salt on their tails. Thenceforth a supply of salt became a regular part of his equipment for a walk. When his cap, his gaiters, and his comforter were all put on, and his gloves had been adjusted to the chubby fingers as a corset might be adjusted to a calf's-foot jelly, he signified that his sport for the day was bird-catching, and was duly supplied with ammunition from the salt-box. He may have thought it was a funny way of catching birds; but " theirs not to reason why," he believed.

Then he set off for the coverts—usually the courtyard of a dear old sleepy Government building near which it was his happiness to live—and, with a pinch from the paper, made for his first bird. The pigeons knew and rather liked him— they have a sort of natural fellow-feeling with innocence—and they would stand anything from him but being caught. They stood the salt without the slightest displeasure, not infrequently bringing their tails into position for the ceremony when they saw that he had nothing for their beaks, and then waddling out of range. He may have wondered how, in face of such difficulties, the race of man contrived to get its pigeons into its pies, but he was still content to give the benefit of the doubt to his elders as the source of all truth.

Wearying of the sport at last, for lack of encouragement, he then began to busy himself with the question—not of his " Whence and whither ? " (the latter belongs to a far more advanced stage of curiosity), but only of the " Whence ? "—and he was duly informed that he had come into the world by the process of digging for him in a strawberry bed. He took it, of course, as another deliverance of the oracle that could not lie; and, without a moment's delay, sought his toyshop for a spade. The strawberry bed was not so easily found, but a forlorn backyard of his old Jacobean residence furnished a sort of garden plot, which he was told—" just to keep him quiet "—might, at a pinch, produce the active principle of strawberry tart as a reward of the labours of husbandry. No miner ever dug for gold with more ardour than our neophyte now began to dig for a swaddled babe, and, after many disappointments, he found what promised to be a pocket at least, though finally it produced nothing but a drowned kitten almost fresh from the pail.

He left off digging, and it would have been well had they followed his example with their lies. But they went from bad to worse. Their next abuse of his confidence was to persuade him that his actions could not possibly escape the vigilance of a certain print gown. The print gown was on the back of a certain young person in charge of him, and its pattern was one of white spots on a background of chocolate. His custodian, by way of turning this circumstance to account, assured him that the spots were so many eyes which beheld his misdeeds as clearly when the wearer's back was turned as when he stood before her face. She had said so, and her mates had aided and abetted her in the cheat. He believed again, though now, as we may infer, he had begun to require corroborative testimony.

For a time, then, her shapely shoulders awed him into virtue as effectually as her regard. But doubts had entered his mind, and one fearful day he put them to the test by playing with the fire, just for the sake of seeing what would come of it. He lit a wisp of paper while she was looking out of window and waving signals to someone in the street. Nothing came of it—nothing at all. He lit another with precisely the same result.

As a last desperate venture he now essayed the unpardonable sin of reaching the mantelpiece, with the aid of a chair, and lighting a match. It scratched as it kindled; it even flared a report, yet still nothing happened, again. He let it burn to the end, the spots staring fixedly at him all the time, and then sat down, hushed with terror, to await the reckoning. The wardress at last turned, her face flushed with pleasure, and closed the window. Yet all that happened, even now, was a kiss, and a promise that he should be taken out at once, as he had been such a very good little boy.

Then he knew for certain that lying was one of the industries of man, and he was visited by his first dim forebodings of a planet of ratepayers. He trampled on the flower bed, bearing his punishment for soiled socks with heroic calm, and threw the salt in their faces when next they made that base offering of homage to his credulity. They thought they had dealt with him after the manner of his folly : they had really dealt after the manner of theirs. He never swallowed them whole from that time forth.

A LITTLE ELBOW ROOM

THE luncheon bell, and the slave of letters in the midst of a happy inspiration : at last the vein had yielded and the blood had begun to flow. The bell put a stop to all that. He rushed to the dining-room, to eat without an appetite and talk without a topic, till the end of the sitting. Then duty suggested a walk, and a visit of digestion, whereat he produced himself in chatter which carried him still further away from the one thing needful. Taking the club on his way home, he met a bore, who, no doubt, thought that the mis-adventure was all his own. Coming back at last to his study, he tried to resume the happy moment —only to find that it was gone. The god, huffed at having been kept waiting, had left the premises.

Then there came to him the idea, as yet un-troubled in its freshness by the pale cast of thought, of an essay on the reopening of Liberty Hall. Think of these trivial interruptions, and then of their multiplication into all the hours of the working day—the breakfast as well as the luncheon, not to speak of afternoon tea, a con-stant something that steps in between you and the things you want to know about and the things you want to do. We seem to have lost the secret of the

earlier men, the thing done just when they wanted
to do it—the " Take me while I'm in the humour,"
as an everlasting motto for the whole business.

A supremely successful portrait painter of my
acquaintance works either in a perfect fury of improvisation or does not work at all. The sitter
has to bear the racket of it, even if the sitter is a
duke. The sketch is done as swiftly as the drawing of a lightning artist at the music-halls, and
if it does not come right the whole thing is anni-
hilated with one sweep of a velveteen sleeve. This
method throws the burden of compliance on the
Muse, by a fierce refusal to have anything to do
with her when she happens to be coy. Muses, it
is said, respond to treatment of this sort.

Those, I think, who work in the arts need this
looser order, like soldiers in the new systems of
drill. The awful regularity of the conditions of
modern production is a fatal hindrance. Everything is done by the clock. It is the artist to his
easel, the writer to his blotting pad, as regularly
as the clerk to his desk, and the result often tells
the tale of the process in every line. When the
advertising tailors brought poetry into puffing,
their bards were rung in with the rest of the hands,
and rung out again for meals. Literary work has
too often to follow suit. The publishers are waiting, the printers waiting, the bookbinders, the
whole gang of production.

Oratory obeys the same law, in order to achieve

the miracle of the modern lecture, the modern sermon. You engage yourself in advance for humour or pathos by dates in the calendar. You mount pulpit or platform, and, whatever your frame of mind, start with the awful feeling that it would be ruin to pause. How are you to answer for yourself? The lecture is perhaps the worse trial—the reverberating hall, probably in an alien town, and the committee lying in wait for your chilling exchange of commonplaces with persons you have never met before, and are never going to meet again. After that, the procession, usually by a sort of ladder stair that recalls the conditions of the scaffold, and the rows of upturned faces and the utter sinking of the heart. One sighs for the freer methods of nature, for something that may restore to the process of utterance the spontaneity of the bird's song.

The inevitable reaction against this is perhaps to the more unconditioned life, and this is, too often, but another way of saying life in some place which is not home. Be it ever so perfect, let 'it not be that—the old song may run that way soon. All the signs point to a great change. The big town establishment is already a thing of the past. The flat has ruined it, and the hotel may serve the flat in the same way. The very Rowton lodging-house is a revolt against unnecessary ties: all of us seem to want fewer meaningless obligations, more elbow room.

Hotel life is nearest to the life of Liberty Hall, the life of the great volitions with a free course. The means are easy, at any rate for authors of fashion who happen to be without encumbrances; and for the rest of us, though it may still come short of the achievement, there can be no harm in making it a longing. The rule is golden, as usual: be not too close with the management about terms, and *see* the chambermaid and the waiter the first thing. That settled, you have taken up your freedom of the establishment; and it is all the life of the green wood. You may go to bed when you like, rise, feed, or fast when you like, see or shun company, ensure absolute respect for all your moods.

It is the life without remonstrance. Your wakeful eye rolls in a fine frenzy at midnight—well, sit it out till the organ blinks at the morning sun. You hunger and thirst during the vigil—it is easy to have refreshments at hand on the side table. Your noble head bows with fatigue at last—it is but a few paces to your bedchamber, and to a dreamless sleep that may persist till noon. A signal will convey your wish for quiet to those who have learned the code. You descend at your own hour, and sure of a meal. If it is their luncheon, it may be your breakfast: the waiter knows, and no other in all the grazing throng.

What is all this but a return to the at least fabled freedom of the forest life, plus fine napery, tactful service, and the range of the meat and drink of the world? Cooked cutlets grow on the trees—for you—and your favourite sauce is wafted to your side, as if by magic, with a touch of the bell. It is Walden Woods, in its independence, with the resources of civilisation thrown in. You escape all obtrusive solicitude, all the partnership of joys and sorrows that so often gives the sorrows so much more than their share. There is no suggestion of a cook on strike in the kitchen, no intrusive recommendation of tasteless courses that are supposed to be for your good.

You are cheerful, with the sense of being ahead of time in having the day's work practically at an end. You are urbane, preventive, courteous, on the true foundations of having done as you please. You are free to think of others, having put away from you, by the simple process of complete satisfaction, all thought of yourself. The rest of the day comes as it may in mere work, if you still feel the hunger for it, in the best communion with the best in your reach, if your taste lies that way. The only good company is the company you can have at will and drop at will. It is a mistake to see too much of anybody: even a wife's own sister is at her best with intervals of experience, like the stars.

So may you live the life of impression, dear to the artist in all kinds. He is eccentric by law, not by a freak. Freedom is the golden rule: to do

D

anything well you must be allowed to do it in your own way. Old Brindley, the engineer, used to think out his canals in bed. Edison saves time on the family meals and the other ordered futilities. I like that fable about his wedding : the hour had come for the ceremony, and the bride was setting out for church, but the man was not at hand. They tracked him to his laboratory, and found him busy with electric storage, and in his working clothes. It was a bad attack of absence of mind.

This is the true Bohemianism, and the only kind that counts, with liberty, not licence, for its end and aim. The Bohemianism of the pot-house is a dead thing : it was hindrance and enslavement, and it had to go. The new sort, even in the humbler reaches, was once happily defined as the clean shirt, though perhaps the clean shirt under difficulties. Freedom for the finer impulses, that is the thing; and of all these grossness is the enemy. So also is the cut and dried. We are afraid to take the first step of the first turning to the land of Do-as-you-Please.

Who that has ever stood at his door at bedtime, to have one peep at the spangled heavens before turning in, has not felt the craving to make a night of it? Why not an occasional ramble till dawn? For no reason in the world, I imagine, but that it has never been done by the man over the way. If there is another, it is only the fear of catching cold. Yet what a thing to forego! The loss may partly be realised by him who has slept in a studio with a top light, or, for that matter, in a garret with a hole in the roof. The great venture would be so easy, but for the fear of your brother parishioner, or of that still more influential fellow creature, a daughter of Eve at your elbow. 'Tis but putting on your hat, and all the open country is yours, in an exquisite radiance that is light both for the eyes and for the soul.

Every dog of us, in his day, has paced the gaslit streets in the small hours, but how few have ventured on a constitutional by the light of the moon! The whole landscape is transformed by it, and all things, the commonest with the rest, seem to breathe the secret of a new significance. The shadows are portals of sibylline caves, the light's gentle strife for mastery with the void of darkness has the majesty of the fiat of creation. The sounds of night birds, insects, footfalls of prowling things, are just as impressive and just as strange. The silver rivers are all tributaries of the River of Eden; the sea, though it may be the sea of the tripper, is the very ocean of being into which they flow; the distant sail, an emblem of the voyage of life. And all within reach of a rate-payer taking a walk.

He may have it pretty much to himself, thanks to mankind's highly cultivated taste for arc-light, and to its fear of catarrh. And if he does not, he will almost to a certainty find himself in good company, since few fail to feel the mystic influences of the hour. His luck will probably take the form of a coastguardsman or a rural constable, but the tramp asleep, with one eye open, under a hedge will do as well as either at a pinch. All have the spirit attuned to that inner sense of the world as a place of peace, which is part of the great secret. The midnight walk ought to be a regimen, I was going to say a diet. There will be a moonlight cure as soon as some quack hits on the idea of charging fifty guineas for the course. It is the cheapness that repels.

Such excursions into our true native country of the silence and the solitude bring the intuitions that are the life of the artist, the writer, the merchant of ideas, no matter what the nature of his wares. We are kept from them by the fear that they may interfere with the work : truly speaking, they are the work—they, and nothing else. The service of all artistry must be the service of perfect freedom. The daily tale of scribbling, painting, fiddling is apt to impoverish the whole output.

Anæmia of the sensations is the worst of all complaints, though I am not sure that you will find it in the books. The spirit has its own times, and the true husbandman in these crafts is the one who waits devoutly on its will. No doubt this was the happy accident of much of the older literature. Poverty and obscurity gave its practitioners their free time in whole swaths, when nobody minded them, and they perforce had to take life as it came. All Goldsmith is implicit in the delightful wanderings in France, when he had nothing in the world but the flute in his pocket to provide bed and breakfast, and rarely took it out in vain.

> Dear happy land of innocence and ease;
> Pleased with thyself, whom all the world can please.
> How often have I led thy festive choir
> With tuneful pipe, beside the wandering Loire !

He carried little more than he stood upright in, yet his baggage of notes may have been precious in the promise of masterpieces to come. Jean Jacques went on tramp for his best thoughts; his study was but the counting house of his impressions. Swift knew what he was about in his occasional flights into the lowest company of his time. Turner's excursions of the same sort were rude strivings of that passion for independence, and of that wise horror of the hackneyed, that were the life of his art. He fled from something that was devitalising, as well as to something that was vile. His pot-houses were not all rapture, but at least no brother painters were at the bar.

Who vagabondises now? Which is as much as to say, Who wisely wanders at will? Our very exercise is the treadmill of a golf-link. We go the rounds of poverty and squalor in the care of a detective, and uniformed for the most part in cast-off weeds of fashion that proclaim our status from the house-tops. The way to see it all properly is, for the time being, to live the life. Even the wonderfully well-informed ministrants of charity lack that resource. They descend from above, returning by the clock to the blessed abodes, and miss things. The true seer must come as the equal and the mate, above all suspicion of a friendship with a purpose, with no particular plan in advance, and wholly at the mercy of the incident. This comes as it may, and kindly chance will be sure to take you where you want to go, there or thereabouts.

For never forget that the detective by appointment really shows you nothing worth seeing, since he is, at best, but the stage manager of a pageant of squalor, and his company have all rehearsed their parts. The way to do it is the Caliph Haroun's way, following the lead of your interest and your curiosity, and, above all, of your pure human interest in other lives. O the delight of getting away from the use and wont of your own set to the use and wont of another! They are conventions both, of course, things made with hands in the shape of circumstance, creations of the public opinion of your social circle, whether they be of the drawing-room or of the slum. The needy knife-grinder is as purely artificial a product as his betters, but, as the new chum, he is a change, and he helps to give you the richer liberty of that wonder world—life as it is lived. Pity there is no social machinery for giving the far east of our great cities an occasional frolic at the other end.

A life-long friend of mine once tried to realise this to fancy with "A Night in Belgrave Square: by a Costermonger." He had to do it for the costermonger, since to do it by him was beyond the bounds of possibility. Our dukes are no longer enterprising, or they would periodically contrive to entertain a Christopher Sly as a part of the comedy of their state. Their next best would be to give him a look in from time to time for themselves; but this duty, this opportunity, they most shockingly neglect.

Our very walks in the country tend to drift into walking tours, announced in advance in the papers, if the nimble paragraphist happens to be in the way. O for the spirit of Borrow, mightiest walker before the Lord, and mightiest spinner of the yarn! The true way is to enter the first railway station, at home or abroad, and ask to be taken as far as your loose silver will frank you, trusting to luck for the rest. The inherent charm of life is sure to begin just wherever they set you down, town or village, ugly or beautiful, excluding only, if you have any choice in the matter, the tabulated picturesque in either kind.

Adventures, in this as in other sorts, are to

the adventurous.   Out you go, and it comes.   We
lack the splendid wastes of Spain, but there are
pickings in modern England, especially if we take
it in the faith that modern and ancient are all one,
and that there, exactly where the foot presses, is
potential fairyland.   We have only to get rid of
the notion that romance is nowhere to be found
but in the remote and strange.   We want a new
birth in this, a birth into the idea that the world
of actuality, with the rawest thing in it, is a peren-
nial wonder.   Distance, whether of time or place—
antiquity, is but a trick of perspective : it is all on
the one plane of delight.   The now and the here
are assuredly on the way to be ten thousand years
old, and they are perfectly good for that effect as
they stand.   By all accounts, we have, if not
countless, at any rate undetermined millions of
years before us; and the end is not yet in sight
of the wisest.

So, with this new thing, this raw thing, we
are already in a very night of the ages, and
Assyrian and Egyptian were really no better off.
The Victorian age is quite hoary, yet how fresh
it seemed but the other day !   Without the power
of realising the past in the present, we are hopelessly lost.   We should be able to reverse for the
standpoint, at a moment's notice.   This day five
hundred years hence everybody will be able to
see the charm of our commonplace, the high and
pure romance, as of a thing in the purposes of

creation, of a penn'orth to the Bank in a mustard-pot omnibus. Why should it be a mere privilege of genius to see it now? So nothing shall prevent us from exchanging new lamps for old, in this fashion, whatever the almanacs may say to the contrary.

Thus seen, surburban villadom itself will be all loveliness and romance, and no longer a mere horror of the actual and a very death of hope. We are afield, and we cannot go wrong. The flannel shirt and the change of hose are in the knapsack; we know not where we may have to sleep, where pull up for the mid-day meal, or where take shelter from the rain. No letters will follow us—if we are wise—and no bags. The last are a vexation of spirit, for they take the work out of the hands of Providence by marking a course. As for the letters, surely the great Napoleon said the decisive word: " Leave them unopened for a week, and most of them will have answered themselves."

This was Borrow's secret, and about the only one. His spirit was that of the great adventurers, the great wanderers, from Ulysses to our day. The character, the incident, never failed to meet or to overtake him. His service to his generation was to show that the humdrum is but a figment of the mind. A thousand before him had gone from the Dan to the Beer-sheba of their day with the cry: " 'Tis all barren ! " He touched it with the wonder glow.

Only last week, in a walk over the hills, I struck a fine old English town that had scarcely stirred in its sleep since the Middle Ages. The houses were of old grey stone; there was grass in the streets, though not too much of it; the comfortable inns called themselves hotels, here and there, but they didn't believe it, nor did they expect such credulity in anybody else. A stroll revealed the existence of a community of handicraftsmen, with Ruskin and Morris for their canon, and for their workshop a building of eld, with an outlook on a fair garden of the same. There they made beautiful things for love, while select purchasers from all the ends of the earth came to wonder, if not quite often enough to buy. As a mere discovery, of course, it was purely personal to myself, but, as the luck of a summer morning, it was no bad thing.

Think of seeing not England alone but France, Italy—the world so. This, again, I am aware, is no original suggestion, though it is still a somewhat unwonted thing. Select souls of the confraternity of the Rücksack often wake the echoes of the Black Forest, the Alp, the Apennine, the plains of the Loire, and what not, in this way. But how small is the Order! For the grosser balance of mankind nothing will serve but the horrors of the Riviera, the big hotel, the bloated Swiss, the table d'hôte where tail-coated Britons glare suspicion of each other's status across the table, the smoking room where they compare records in pigeon shooting and golf.

The weary and the wearisome souls! For all of it is so sedulously contrived to be just nothing at all—not native country, since it lacks the dear homeland note; and assuredly not foreign, since it has the universality that precludes all note whatsoever. At best it is but a sort of Gordon's land— the Company, alas! and not the hero—which is no man's land in being every man's, the region of the Grand Tour through the Inane.

In such scenes of travel nothing happens but catalogued ruins, emporiums of bric-à-brac, or, at best, for the crises of experience, garlic in the mutton, or an underdone chop. Even the last is rare in the monotony of their insipid perfections. We are still waiting for unity in faith, but we have at last achieved a catholicity of potage and of sauce. Its worst result is a separation of classes never known before.

Our fathers perforce mixed more with their kind, at home and abroad. The coach and, above all, the public highway, were great levellers; and if the chariot secured a savage isolation for the few, there was always the higgledy-piggledy of the inn. The waggon on which Roderick Random came to town was a perfect epitome of character and of adventure. The canal boat, which marked a step in advance, was pulsing life in everything but the speed.

The syndicated hotel has effected a social segregation which might give points to the caste systems of the East. Here are the classes; the masses are hardly so much as in sight. There is a universal guest, a universal waiter, a universal bill of fare, a universal feature of the landscape, varied a little as to localities, but still in the sealed pattern, like all the rest. The people of the country, their habits, tastes, manners, and customs never intrude. The nearest approach to the peasant is the hotel gardener—in uniform—or the wench that brings the milk, and she steals in by the back way.

For a' that and a' that, Liberty Hall is less hospitable than it seems. For whom is this freer life to be revived? For the artist, or for his neighbours as well—the soldier, the doctor, the lawyer, the man of affairs, the man at the plough? Might not they put in their claims? And, if they did, would not the last state of the apostle of freedom be worse than the first? Punctuality is notoriously the soul of business, and, if rules were broken at will, the shock might be too much for the framework of things. The day's government must be carried on, whatever betide. Think of impressionist hot rolls at midday, the baker only turning up after prolonged orisons, nay, perhaps prolonged oblations overnight. Think of impressionist trains, running at the sweet will! How the man of letters and the rest of the clan would write to the papers! The sweet-willers are apt to want everything to order but their own lives, and the culture they represent might easily, like the Athenian, become a beauty of life dependent on slave labour.

Once more, what about the others? Perhaps we have no right to put the question. Some people are not " the others." There are classes apart, categories that demand special treatment— if you will, like the insane. The alternative term for them is a priesthood consecrated to the life of impulse, of whim, of the something that is not convention. The claim is not necessarily so presumptuous as it seems. Theirs may simply be the modest function to show that, with all its rightful empire over souls, convention is not quite absolutely the all in all. Its mastery would still be confessed by their service, as was that of the old *Spectator's* " Muley Moloch, Emperor of Morocco," by the slave's warning that he was still mortal. It was but the cry of his chattel, and it was still a tribute to his greatness and to his power.

For great is convention, and great is order, and great is the hand of the clock; and, in the main, these things must ever rule life. The gentle Bohemian is only for the days of the saturnalia, and as the exception that proves the rule. He is but the glove of velvet for the iron hand, and of iron the hand of our governance, whether our own or another's, must ever be. A life of go-as-you-please—the foolish Anarchists have dreamed of such a thing—would land us in chaos. Life is a bitter business. Take it as such, hard and early, yet pity the unhappy few who, by their nature, are doomed to take it the other way. They are but moths at best, and most of them perish of their passion for freedom and light.

This part of the question might absorb an essay all to itself, but the essay will have to wait. To tell the truth, the mere scratching of the pen has begun to get on the present writer's nerves, and he is going to take the first train for Nowhere in Particular.

To be continued to-morrow or next week or never; the cab is at the door.

BIG BOOKS FOR LITTLE PEOPLE

My favourite books, as one of the Little People, are the books that console my compulsory vigils of the night, and soften the rigour of my expiation of the fault of dining out. It is notorious that the worst punishment of this delinquency is the abundant opportunity it affords for reflection on the follies of a lifetime. Here my bedside books come in as giving me something better to think of. They are soothing in time of trouble, and at other times good comrades and sharers of joy. Of the thousand thousand other books, most excellent in their way, even of those that send one to sleep in spite of oneself, there will be nothing said here.

Two great writers have discovered or explored the " human boy "; my humble theme is the human book. This book is emphatically the book that touches my feelings, whether to mirth or sadness, and makes me feel good. Mind, I do not say virtuous: I mean good in the American sense of the phrase—touched with the beauty of life, one with the sympathetic magnetisms of the world. The world is sometimes so cold, and I am sometimes just as bad as the world; in either case it is pleasant to have the books at hand.

Our coldness, I think, comes in great part of

our strenuousness. We overdo the mood of con-
fliet until the enemy gets on our nerves, and we see
Birnam Wood in every clump. We are wont to
affect the passions of the fabled prime when the
strong clutched, and the weak let go and waited
for the leavings. Our prophets are Schopenhauer
and Nietzsche, our literature, even of the imagina-
tion, is a thing of cut and slash—a reaction perhaps against an earlier diet of the amenities carried
too far into our teens. Yet peace and quietness of
taste are not dead; they are only in hiding, and
there are moments when their devotee longs to
steal out and visit them in their caves. Then the
big books for Little People have their turn.

Come to me, then, my " Cranford," from the
shelf where I keep my bedside books, the books
that are not to send me to sleep, but to help me
to find it with a quiet mind; or otherwise, if perforce I must keep wakeful, to exorcise the demons
of the night. I know where my copy is sure to
open—at the sketch of the women making all
safe for the night. The doors are bolted, the windows clasped; there remains but the final search
for the burglar. To look would be too dreadful;
but there is an easier test. Throw this tethered
ball under the bed and draw it back again; if it
finds no resistance either way, the house is safe.

It is the woman's touch in humour, with quite
a quality of its own, free from all horseplay and
violence of effect. The entire settlement of old

maids, most of them still young in body and soul, with its sweet and simple outlook on life, is pictured in the stroke. Under its influence one will presently drop off, not with a yawn of boredom, but with the feeling that the world is still a habitable place with many a sheltered nook.

Sterne's Widow Wadman is just in the same order of effects. The widow, you remember, feels sure that she can bring Uncle Toby to the point, if only she can induce him to look her full in the face. To this end she implores him to aid her in the discovery of a mote in her eye. Uncle Toby is saved by his simplicity. " I protest, madam, that I see nothing in your eye." " The Vicar of Wakefield " would have served my purpose just as well—in the scene of the horse-thief masquerading as a sage. "And yet, sir, the cosmogony or creation of the world," etc. I quote from memory in each case, but I think I am pretty near the mark.

A stronger, not to say a coarser, effect would I fear be out of place. Mark Twain, for instance, would be too full of energy, not to say too mechanical in some of his flights. Gambetta, I believe, always kept Rabelais as a bedside book. The joyous one is all very well, but his laugh is too much of the Homeric cast for the sense of repose. I say nothing of passages that are no more conducive to that frame of mind than a Channel passage. The mood for the midnight

E

hour is perfect peace. And when that has been denied, and you put forth your hand in the darkness before switching on the light, it should always fall on a book of the right sort.

Benson must rank here in spite of the actuality of his date. His " College Widow " gives an outlook on a good-fellowship of the spirit that is under no tyranny of time. He is of that society of friends who, as he says, " will value more and more books that speak to the soul rather than books that appeal to the ear and the mind. They will realise that it is through wisdom and force and nobility that books retain their hold upon the hearts of men, and not by briskness and colour and epigram. A mind thus stored may have little grasp of facts, little garniture of paradox and jest, but it will be full of compassion and hope and gentleness and joy." Agreed.

" Be not too clever " might be written up on the Temple of Fame : more are shut out, I fancy, by neglect of that caution than by dullness itself. So Borrow shall be a member of my ancient and honourable society, if only for the sake of his work in Spain, perfect as travel, perfect as atmosphere of romance, perfect, too, with rare exceptions in its freedom from literary artifice.

These are the friendly books; the sweet and tender come in hand with " The Pearl," that beautiful old poem in the Middle English, whereof the authorship has vanished into the night of things. It is all the dearer to me for that. One likes to think of it as a completed transaction, the actual writer not personally available in any way for details of birthplace or history or collected works, not even in the disembodied state of a line in a biographical dictionary. His complete indifference in this respect only makes you the more ready to praise in the fullest measure.

To ask nothing is to have the larger meed. We have libraries of many sorts as publishing ventures: who will complete the list with a collection in honour of that prolific writer "Anon."? —the frontispiece a solitary mound that might stand for an unknown grave. "The Pearl" has long been very dear to me. Its concept is one of the sweetest in our literature. The peasant father has lost his little girl: he goes to her grave to bewail his loss, falls asleep, and has a vision of her in glory. I quote from Mr. Coulton's modernised version :—

> All glistering white her tunic is,
> Open at sides, and bound between
> With marguerites, I well devise,
> Of purest ray and most serene ;
>> Her sleeves were loose and large, I ween,
>> Inwrought with double gems so white ;
>> Her kirtle was of self-suit sheen,
>> With precious pearls around bedight.

It is her uniform of Paradise; and presently, with her good help, he will catch a glimpse of the heavenly city :—

> Even as it met the Apostle's sight,
> Saw I that city of great renown,
> The New Jerusalem, royally dight
> As it was let from heaven adown.
> Its bulwarks burned with gold so bright,
> As burnished glass that gleams around,
> With noble gems all underpight,
> And pillars twelve on their bases bound.

As I have said elsewhere, rather a Hatton Garden heaven, but with such writing catchy criticism has no place. It was the heaven of its time.

This and Skelton's "Philip Sparrow" have long been within everybody's reach. The last narrowly missed being the finest of its kind in our language. The poet's sparrow was dead, and he bewailed his loss—that would have been enough. But he could not restrain the passion for the conceits that were his bane. He forgot his sorrow, his genuine sorrow, in a dismal attempt to show his cleverness; and then he went all to pieces. For all that, he has given us many an incomparable line.

The less known things in this order are the newly published "Early English Lyrics," between Chaucer and the Elizabethans. This is a fine piece of work, almost in its kind like some bold supplementary voyage of an old navigator who finds another cantle of a new world to add to a half already found. The land it finds in our literature is Merrie England. Here is the dear, long-lost note of our race—humanness as distinct from mere soaring heroism. Our best of fairies is Robin Goodfellow, and our Robin Hood might change names with him and still be the same man. Open this book where you will, and you strike this strain of the sheer good-fellow glorified. In one of its delightful lyrics the lover wants to show that he feels no pain but the pain inflicted by the loved one, not even the anguish of a corn.

> Though love do me so mikell woe,
>   I love you best, I make a vow,
> That my shoe bindeth my little toe,
>   And all my smart it is for you,
>   Forsoothe, methinketh it will me slo,
> But ye sumwhat my sorrow slake,
>   That barefoot to my bedde I go,
> And when I sleep I may not wake.

We are still reading according to the law of my moods; and, it may be, that to this mood for the merely sweet and tender may succeed the craving for the freedom of the wilds of fancy. I have friends at hand for such excursions on my book-shelf : here is " The Arabian Nights." It shares with the others that quality of the atmosphere of emancipation which, I take it, is almost the essential note of all good literature. One longs at times for the great open country of the soul, where all men, women, and events escape the common limitations of our lot, and are superlative, in their several kinds, in character, feelings, passion, circumstance, and never to be caught in the trammels of conditioned being except with their own consent.

This night it may be my high privilege to be out for a frolic in Bagdad as on a certain Midsummer Night I go for a frolic in all Nature. It is the height of the glory of the Caliphate, when trembling millions look towards the capital and its canopy of stars for omens of their fate. Meanwhile its master has slipped away from his throne and his flatterers to realise himself in his slums, amid porters, hunchbacks, cobblers, and duennas, or in the mysteries of closed gardens with a back door for their chief portal, and gorgeous palaces, including his own, which seem all back stairs.

Such excursions are peculiarly for the bookish man, the timid one, the unenterprising, for whom Bradshaw and Baedeker bear no message, and who for the reality of the thing could hardly get as far as the suburbs without a week's packing and a final codicil to his will. A page opens at random beneath his touch, and he leaps leagues and centuries at a bound in space or time. The traveller of real life is apt to have no adequate sense of his opportunities, and to bring back no report worth a moment's attention.

Who has not known what it is to encounter one of these persons fresh from the land of Prester John without being able to get anything more out of him than an essay on the true art of boiling

rice or on the tariffs of hotels. Yet what more
could you expect? he has travelled on wheels instead of wings, and has had his fancy clogged with
a thousand importunities of incident which are no
part of the true business of the soul. But when
the Caliph and I are out for a flutter together, it is
all the pure rigour of the game of fancy, and in a
twinkling we find ourselves in the garden of Noor
Ed-Deen.

" The gate was arched, and over it were vines
with grapes of different colours, the red like rubies,
and the black like ebony. They entered a bower,
and found within it fruits growing in clusters and
singly, and the birds were warbling their various
notes upon its branches. The nightingale was
pouring forth its melodious sounds, and the turtle-
dove filled the place with its cooing, and the black-
bird in its singing resembled a human being, and
the ringdove a person exhilarated by wine. The
fruits upon the trees, comprising every description
that was good to eat, had ripened; and there were
two of each kind: there were the camphor apricot
and the almond apricot and the apricot of Kura-
san; the plum of a colour like the complexion of
beauties, the cherry delighting the sense of every
man; the red, the white, and the green fig of the
most beautiful colours; and flowers like pearls and
coral; the rose, whose redness put to shame the
cheeks of the lovely; the violet, like sulphur in
contact with fire; the myrtle, the gilliflower, the

lavender, and the anemone; and their leaves were bespangled with the tears of the clouds. The camomile smiled, displaying its teeth, and the narcissus looked at the rose with its negroes' eyes; the citrons resembling round cups, the limes were like bullets of gold, the ground was carpeted with flowers of every colour, and the place beamed with the charms of spring; the river murmured by while the birds sang, and the wind whistled among the trees; the season was temperate, and the zephyr was languishing."

And by-and-bye of a certainty—though I know not what is coming and care less—I shall meet company of the right sort to give me triumphant vindication of my refusal of the dinner at Bayswater for this very night. Compare any possible luck in pairing for the dining-room in that region with what has just befallen me on the banks of the Tigris, in an encounter entirely unforeseen.

"She had a mouth like the seal of Suleyman, and hair blacker than the night of estrangement is to the afflicted, and a forehead like the new moon of the festival of Ramadan, and eyes resembling the eyes of the gazelles, and an aquiline nose, and cheeks like anemones, and lips like coral, and teeth like pearls strung on necklaces of native gold, and a neck like molten silver above a figure like a willow branch."

Really, you know!

The Irish talk of a broth of a boy; well, here is a broth of a girl. She takes the floor. Her high strain of perfect freedom from the limitations of earth is almost unattainable by a modern, but it has been well nigh achieved by the author of " A Digit of the Moon " (Parker), a retired Indian civil servant masquerading as a poet of the Golden Age. His delicious parody of the Eastern mind might almost pass the test of the bazaars. It tells of a king woman-hater who was cured of his infirmity on the homœopathic principle of a dose of womanly disdain. The story of how he was humbled, and then exalted again by the glance of forgiveness, which he had hardly deserved, is the high water-mark of fanciful extravagance. Its flashes of fine writing are just as good.

" In the beginning, when Twashtri came to the creation of woman, he found that he had exhausted his materials in the making of man, and that no solid elements were left. In this dilemma, after profound meditation, he did as follows: He took the rotundity of the moon, and the curves of creepers, and the clinging of tendrils, and the trembling of grass, and the slenderness of the reed, and the bloom of flowers, and the lightness of leaves, and the tapering of the elephant's trunk, and the glances of deer, and the clustering of rows of bees, and the joyous gaiety of sunbeams, and the weeping of clouds, and the fickleness of the winds, and the timidity of the hare, and the vanity

of the peacock, and the softness of the parrot's
bosom, and the hardness of adamant, and the
sweetness of honey, and the cruelty of the tiger,
and the warm glow of fire, and the coldness of
snow, and the chattering of jays, and compound-
ing all these together, he made woman, and gave
her to man."

After this dish of sugared foolishness, of
course, one longs for stronger diet, since our entire
race is only less variously compounded than the
young woman of the story. All the moods of the
spirit are in each of us by turns, from saint
and hero to the mere smugness of the ratepayer by
his fireside. The ratepayer is not always in dress-
ing-gown and slippers; and anon, in fancy at
least, he rises to reach for armour on the wall,
though it may be but the spoil of the old curiosity
shops. Emerson and Thoreau are, for these
moments, with Marcus and Epictetus, above all. I
love the cynic of Walden Pond for his note of
mockery of the shows of life.

" Time is but the stream I go a-fishing in. I
drink at it; but while I drink I see the sandy
bottom and detect how shallow it is. Its thin
current slides away, but eternity remains. I would
drink deeper; fish in the sky, whose bottom is
pebbly with stars. I cannot count one. I know
not the first letter of the alphabet. I have always
been regretting that I was not as wise as the day
I was born."

Marcus is especially dear to me, because all the philosophy of the modern schools is implicit in him. You are what you choose to think you are; and you are not anything, however disagreeable, that you may choose to unthink. You affirm and you deny, according to your sovereign will, and so you make your life. Thus the old Roman Emperor, and thus his master the Greek slave of Rome. The latter, indeed, never troubled to write a word of it, but his disciples caught some precious fragments of his gospel of Dogged as they fell from his lips. His thrifty modern successors in Christian and in Mental Science have improved on this, with their warnings against the infringement of copyright in their stolen property—sometimes at the head of every page.

What a fine shop for fine thought, with frontage in the best thoroughfares, either of these pagan sages might have kept in our time. Think of Marcus dressing his window with such maxims as these: " Pain is either an evil to the body— then let the body say what it thinks of it—or to the soul; but it is in the power of the soul to maintain its own serenity and tranquillity, and not to think that pain is an evil. For every judgment and movement and desire and aversion is within, and no evil ascends on high." Every bit of him is of the same quality.

" Short, then, is the time which every man lives, and small the nook of the earth where he lives; and short, too, the longest posthumous fame."

I showed this to a valued literary friend, whose standing grievance was that they had given him a quarter of an inch too little in the current books of reference, and he was good enough to assure me that it had done him good. An hour after I found him raging over a bad review, but what o' that!

" It is royal to do good and to be abused."

" From Rusticus I learned not to be led astray to delivering little hortatory orations, nor to showing myself off as a man who practises much discipline; and to abstain from rhetoric and fine writing."

But the tension of such teaching cannot be kept up for ever. The soul can hardly fetch its breath on these mountain tops. There is a middle region still high above the plain, and with mankind still as pigmies below where à Kempis is the guide, or, better still, perhaps, the divine quietist Mólinos —peaceful, contemplative, receptive to all the finer magnetisms of being. I read these, not merely for their teaching, but, paradoxically perhaps, as autobiography. Precepts of conduct, those trumpet notes of literature might, if not too curiously considered, be regarded as in some sort clues to the character of their authors. Marcus, I daresay, wrote his maxims just because he was the man who stood most in need of them. They were produced for his own consumption, in the first place, and for ours only in the second. They sprang out of his sense of imperfection, not of his sense of mastery. Otherwise we might never have had a word about the matter. They show him as what he was, or at least as what he wanted to be. His counsels were confessions, in spite of him.

On this theory one might estimate à Kempis as naturally a proud man, since he is so everlastingly concerned with the axiom of humility. Only a fool, of course, would call him a hypocrite on that account. It was the cry of his sincere conviction of the necessity for a change of heart from the excesses of spiritual pride. Humble me, humble me, make me less sure of my own progress in grace, is the dominant note throughout. "Take heed of vain pleasing of thyself and of pride. Be not proud of well-doing . . . it is very prejudicial to thee to prefer thyself to any man . . . The learned are well pleased to seem so to others and to be accounted wise."

What else can it all mean? Such a method of interpretation is no doubt to be used with caution or it would be too cheap in its results. One would only have to turn an ethical formula inside out to be entitled to charge the moralist with all the faults of the seamy side, and to judge saint and sage with fatal facility out of his own mouth. In this way our great essayist of decision of character would be self-convicted of being unstable as water, and every Stoic would stand confessed a self-coddling valetudinarian. Yet what surprises of this kind are in the autobiographical fragments of Carlyle ! The persistency of the note of aspiration is sometimes a disquieting sign. As a rule, those who have a quality, like those who have a thing, take it very much as a matter of course, and seldom make it the subject of their confidences or their prayers.

The " Bhagavad " (of the Temple Classics by preference) is for this region, and, with its help, we shall find the blest Krishna and Arjuna still in their divine communion in the things that count, in a strain of compliment worthy of a god and a high-bred devotee.

The book was written to reconcile a speculative race to the life of action. They were all shrinking from works, that is to say, from doing anything, and were laying the whole stress on meditation as a way of attaining to perfect one-ship with the divine. The poet-author seems to have felt that something must be done to modify their disdain of deeds—hence the Dialogue. Krishna tells the inquirer that there are two ways of attaining blessedness, and he graciously permits the battle and the march.

But here would come in a difficulty for Brahmanical adepts. What could be more odious than action in and for itself and to mere worldly ends ? The corrective is that it must be performed as an act of sacrifice, and with an absolute indifference to other issues. One is reminded of the devotees of another faith who tend the sick not so much to cure the patient as to cure their own souls. This, by keeping the mind still in a sort of detachment from the world, will effect the needful reconciliation between faith and works. Detachment saves the principle : you offer your tribute of action on the shrine of the god, and leave it there, without the slightest concern as to what he means to do with it. The action is for the offering, not the offering for the action. This should bring much comfort, and especially that of a healthy indifference to success or gratitude. It is about the only thing that will enable us to work strenuously in the void of good intent.

" Passion and loathing . . . one should not come under the sway of these twain, for they are foes in the path. . . . Casting off all the works upon me with thy mind in the One over Self, be then without craving and without thought of a Mine, and put away thy fever and thy fight."

This is Krishna's " supreme word deepest of all " ; and it is most thankfully received.

" My bewilderment has vanished away; I have gotten remembrance by thy grace, O Never-Falling. I stand freed from all doubt. I will do thy word."

These are my friends in high ethical romance. I will not say that I take them for mere precept : they are not a code, they are an influence, a soft persuasion, a something around me and about me, awaiting me in their better moments and in mine. Sometimes I take the liberty of laughing at them as fogies; and I call them dreamers when they threaten to thwart me in a chosen course. But, just because I can take such liberties with them, they are all the dearer to me : for deep down in my heart there is honour, love, reverence for their high imaginings, and faith that these will one day be made good as lamps to the feet of human experience. I daresay they sometimes laughed at themselves. The author of the " Bhagavad " perhaps had drunk of some potion not of earthly brew, and was, even to his own consciousness, a little strange. The very innocency of some of them, at which we can all smile, is also, I think, a part of their heroic equipment.

Such books are so many varieties of living humanity—and I go to one or the other according to the mood of the moment. It is possible to need them all in the course of a night and a day—so rapid are the changes of cloud formation in the mind as it catches the sun or the wind. I make no apology for the changes, hardly even in the sense of any explanation of them. At one moment you are for Chaucer's company in the frolic sense of the morning and the springtime beauty of life. At another you are for Dr. Thomas Browne of Norwich and the cumulative grandeur of his thought on all things earthly and divine. So of the rest.   All men surely are in each man; and the spirit of man, in mere sympathy and without a thought of toleration, is ready to understand them all.   Hence, perhaps, a certain inconstancy in the moods, if not, as I hope, in the character of those whose calling is the business of interpretation.

There are some, no doubt, who find themselves incapable of making this allowance.   They know exactly what they think and are going to think about everything; and their yesterday, to-day and to-morrow of the spirit are all one.   I neither envy nor blame: it is enough if, purely in the course of business, I have arrived at some perception of their point of view.   They are an order and a classification; and potent indeed in human affairs.   Maybe they sometimes find one another uninteresting—I hope so—but that, perhaps, is less of a conviction than a solace for wounded self-respect.

I have said something elsewhere of the risk of having general views of the great practical concerns of life, and have made what I consider the handsome admission that an impressionistic guide-book would never do.   Short views and limited views are for action; and action is still a chief end of man, if not, as some insist, the only one. Reading is apt to become a kind of dram-drinking, and the courage it induces is often but Dutch courage at the best.

Hence, no doubt, our widespread suspicion of

F

the studious class. They tend to fade away at the point of contact with the trials of life; they launch an epigram or two, shrug their shoulders, and yield the floor.

It is astonishing, it is almost disheartening, to an amateur of ideas to see with what a meagre equipment of that kind the world's work is carried on. He meets the great soldier, statesman, nay, even the great thinker or the great apostle, only to be amazed by the want of variety in their stock-in-trade. They are each pushing one article—the soldier, some happy, strategical combination, or tactical move, not much more subtle than the trick of a master of fence; the statesman, some simple issue that appeals to all and gives them a common property of a cry; the philosopher, or the divine, a system which is often the narrowest thing of all, and commends itself by the ease with which it may be packed in a carpet bag. Our collector of ideas often bewilders by a too abundant choice of wares; and he displays them without winning so much as the tribute of an interjection.

Yet ideas are beautiful things for all that; and little people as well as great live by them—the former mainly as they live by the fresh air, in small doses warranted not to give cold in the head. These, perhaps, are the wiser: the poor " sensitive " who responds to all the vibrations of the ether, suffers their attendant torments, in his tremulous and too responsive soul.

FAILURES

IDEAS often make for ill-luck, though they are not exactly a sole cause of the unread, the unacted, the unbought, the unwanted in all the arts. Will anyone write the tragedy of the Failures? Hardly: it might raise a riot in the house. Dante should have given them a circle to themselves, if, indeed, he had not already made a whole book the story of their woes. For all his tabulated sinners have so hopelessly missed it in love and war and life at large, and ever by a sort of doom that is none of their seeking. The failures suffer as their law of being, and their sharpest pang must be the occasional laughter, as of mocking Olympians, that comes from the seats where the happy fellows who have hit it are enthroned. Many of them work so hard, and cultivate so many of the minor virtues of greatness—in vain, for want of the root of the matter.

One such I knew in my student days at the art school. He was a clerk, and a clerk in middle life, worse luck, who had suddenly made up his mind to become a painter. His idea of the way to do it was to copy masterpieces—not to initiate them, but to copy. He copied accordingly, like a busy lens, light for light, shadow for shadow, line for

line; all transferred from some brilliantly im-
provised original to his laboured sheet. Nothing
came of it, as may be supposed, but he could never
see that nothing was to come.

Little people with but half his count of years
would do more in a minute with one happy turn
of the hand than he in a long procession of hours.
I asked him once where he was going to spend his
Christmas. " Drawing in my bedroom," he cried
fiercely; " art is Christmas enough for me." I'm
not sure that in practical achievement he ever got
so far as valentines. The other day one more of
the same exalted order of the doomed was found
dead in a garret—his only furniture four boxes
filled with rejected manuscripts from all parts of
the world. Why do the high gods fool us so?
If I had the making of the world I think—but
never mind that.

An inquest on the contents of the boxes would
probably have been more to the purpose than the
inquest on the dead man. Why this impulse to
produce, blameless in itself, this stirring of the sap
to such paltry issues? Why a light so treacherous
to give the lead? If it had been an impulse to
crime, one might be able to dismiss the case with
an " I told you so," and a smile of content. But
an impulse to creative endeavour, so often a matter
of garlands and of public applause! What a
mystery it all is.

The note of the failure is unteachableness, a

royal obstinacy in futile courses, and, over and
above this, a disposition to lay all the blame on the
circumstances. Yet, who laid all the folly on him?

I pause only to ask the question, and I pass on.
The circumstances have never been ideally right
for him. But for one thing or other he would have
come off splendidly: he has "never had a fair
start"—when you hear that, you may put him in
his pigeon-hole at once. This refusal to take the
hand as it is dealt, and make the best of it, this
everlasting quarrel with the cards, is decisive.
Cursed spite that he was born poor while the other
man was born rich. And so on. Common
casuistry is but horseplay beside the ingenuity
of this type in demonstrating its utter want of
opportunity: it never reaches its last plea.

But why dwell on the fault when the penalty is
so hard to bear. This everlasting sense of contrast
between the other man's flukes and your own
misses must be the very creeping paralysis of
character. If your difficulty were but an accident
of birth, fixed and unalterable, like a too aspiring
or a too pushful nose, it might admit of the solace
of resignation. But, as an ordered sequence and
recurrence of mischance in every venture, it must
gall like a burden of fate. It seems to bespeak a
watchful vigilance of malignant powers that makes
for despair, and more effectually because hope still
has time to lift its head in the intervals of the
strokes.

The perfect society would be one in which everybody had the place suited to his powers, and the honour of his place. We are all Miltons in our passion for praise; and so-called incompetents are as much discouraged by the want of it as the others. It is the true breath of life. The praise, then, and not only that—a share of the pudding too. The present distribution of rewards in both kinds is the worst sign of a mad world. Why do our efficients demand such monstrous and altogether indigestible helps of the pride of life? An opera singer warbles a few notes into the gramophone—merely to clear his throat—and is instantly dowered in royalties with a sum equivalent to a substantial annuity.

There is no rational relation between service and reward as things go, no approach to the finer doctrine that a man's best of social service, as the best he has to give, should be accounted to him for honour and profit in reasonable measure for all his needs. Our saviours, hereditary or other, charge too much: a successful genius fluttering his dividend warrant in our faces is a sorry sight. The surplus of faculty should be the possessor's own affair, a reason for deep thankfulness that he has it in him to do so much for so little, but not a thing to appraise in any values of glory or pelf. For that matter, how are you going to appraise it? If in mere millions, how much would be a living wage for a Leonidas or a Joan of Arc? It would be bad enough if we tried to reckon justly in that way, and to reward true service in equivalents of pounds, shillings, and pence. But think of the chaotic absurdity between Burns's bits of lean as gauger of Excise and some of the bits of fat in the Pension List of his day.

Never shall I forget a certain dinner at one of the literary clubs, in which the favourite of the hour celebrated his twelfth edition and its duplicates in the Western world. On the strength of these he had just sold for eight hundred guineas a short story written in a couple of hours. He felt, I think, that it behoved him to do something in return, and he accordingly fed some of his fellow creatures. He was a good soul, and he was chargeable with nothing worse than the indiscretion of a kindly nature in having invited an old friend of former days to the feast. This one had begun by writing his heart out in fine philosophic disquisitions, which nobody wanted, and in a couple of tragedies in blank verse, which, in his own estimation, represented a sporting offer to the genius of popularity.

It was the fable of the town and country mouse paraphrased into the higher scale of being—a dinner of sixteen covers at something in pounds per head. The country mouse came from no farther afield than a suburb, but, as absolutes admit of no comparison, it was quite as remote as Saturn in its relation to the present scene.

He had declined to all sorts of compromises, on the failure of the double event, and he was now thrall to a publisher. He wrought all sorts of things into volumes with the aid of paste and scissors—travel, adventure, history, poetry for the fireside and the country walk. He sub-edited the very magazine to which the other had contributed the eight hundred and forty pounder. His labours brought him in about a farthing a minute, as against the seven sovereigns of minted gold earned in that period by his old chum. It was the difference between the tweedledum of success in the market and the tweedledee of its opposite.

For this he toiled a good ten hours a day, not unhelped by a devoted wife, who, in the intervals of her attention to the latest baby, hunted up his references and made the paste. She had evidently pressed the dog's-eared collar of his dress coat, and freshened up the silk before sending him forth. There was a strange, furtive look in his eye when a bird, one of the minor incidents of the banquet, was plumped on his plate. I knew that he wanted to steal it, and wrap it up in the *menu* and take it home to her. But we were all too sharp for him, especially the waiter in silk and plush, who had him in charge.

That *menu!*—was there ever to be an end of it —oysters and *chablis;* plump *châteaubriand* gushing nutriment and delectation with each touch of the knife; magnums, each like an urn of some river god irrigating a desert with champagne; interludes of iced sherbet fortified with scented spirit, to refresh the palate for the savoury and the final bouts; *café* and *chasse-café*. His preference I noticed was for the green liqueur, as though for something that might haply kill. The cigars bulked as trunks of trees, and some of them were embalmed in glass.

When last seen he was fighting his way into a last omnibus, regardless of sex or age. How gladly would I have given him his whole fare in pennies for his thoughts. There is no moral—absolutely none: it was merely the difference between good hap and bad hap in the trickiest' of all the arts.

AN OLD STUPID

ANOTHER sort of failure is, or was, a humble friend of mine who was a martyr to an ideal of shop-keeping.

I suppose he was one of the stupidest old fellows that ever lived. Nature had not been kind: his eyes were too close together, the head was too small to give him a fair chance. You could see that, as he stood at the door of his most grievous little second-hand furniture shop, and he was on view there every day—a second-hand human being.

There was little in his shop that was worth taking as a gift, and he had ticketed everything at fancy prices which were the despair of the customer. A deal table, lacking a leg, was marked " The Real Old Sort, 15/-" while you could have had a perfectly sound one, brand new, round the corner, for twelve. He knew nothing of that: he never went round the corner. He just stuck there, in his den, from morn to eve, or picked his way among the piled rubbish that made short work of the scant allowance of light. His only recreations were shifting the stock and labelling it at these prices of Eastern fable.

His good old wife helped him in these proceedings, staggered with him under excessive handicaps of weight for their time of life, breathed no word of her fatigue to anybody, least of all to him, and affected a belief in his star as a tradesman and a ratepayer, which she must have long ceased to feel. They had little more to hope or to fear from that quarter, being both within easy reach of their three score and ten.

His faith in his prices was not to be shaken: it was part of his religion. He thought that he and his country were being ruined by cheap foreign labour in imported deals, and that it was his mission to stand out for their common rights. He therefore referred every derelict in his stock back to a certain golden age of fair profits on the cost of production; and this, with a scanty deduction for wear and tear, fixed the price. It was misleading, especially since the wear and tear was chiefly of his own doing, as he and his feeble partner struggled forth with the goods every morning, and back with them every night. In this way the table had lost its leg by a cannon with a chest of drawers, which also had forfeited a knob in the encounter. The portmanteaux resisted best, yet even they mildewed under the rains of winter, and cracked under the summer suns. It was exasperating to see them at this stage ticketed " All the Go—10/6."

The wayfarer smiled and passed on. The brother shopkeeper treated these effusions in the

literature of the label with the same bemused contempt—contempt touched with pity, for the writer
was still one of the clan. All were engaged in the
same struggle to keep their heads above water at
the expense of their fellow creatures, only this one
had lost the trick of the stroke. He labelled on.

It was his service of the ideal. He was a poet
of human relations, like every one of us in his way.
His ideal was the tradesman and the ratepayer
sufficient to himself and to his country. As a ratepayer he confessedly made default. The policeman regularly left the notices for " currents " and
arrears, though his errand did not preclude the
kindly word. The defaulter was usually saved by
a timely loan. The truth is his belief in himself
as one who ought to be kept going for the good of
the community, hypnotised his fellow creatures.
With the loan, he paid something on account and
then went on exactly as before. He had no sense
of deception in these proceedings; and it would be
hardly an exaggeration to say that he did it all for
the benefit of his class. He was an institution;
and what would become of us all, if we let him go
by the board?

He was true to all the old loyalties, especially
the loyalties of faith. Whatever happened, he
managed to keep up his membership of his chapel.
He hung notices of its services and its modest
festivals in his window, and sold the sermons of
his favourite preacher, or sometimes gave them

away. He was all trust in a redeeming justice for the middleman on this side of the stars, and in a full compensation to come. It was touching to see him and his wife at the Sunday service, looking quite presentable from the waist upwards, the only part visible.

When times were very hard, you might catch them leaving before the collection, but not often. They generally slipped something in the plate, if it were only their last copper coin; and so, after holding their own for the sermon and the raptures of the final hymn, they were left chatting with other respectable people at the chapel door. The rest was a mystery. Sometimes I fancy it took the form of a sardine, in lieu of a joint, for dinner, and butterless bread for tea. Their eating and drinking were generally of this cast. The poor old wife cooked strange compounds at the back of the shop by the light of a paraffin lamp, and sometimes I suspect, when coal was dear, by its warmth, while he read to her books from the stock, labelled " All this lot 2d." It should, of course, have been 1d.: his megalomania of prices betrayed him at every turn.

That was at the root of the whole difficulty. He was an old stupid, incalculably blind, foolish, unaware. Things passed before him as in a dream of human and cosmic relations. He seemed to have done everything wrong from the cradle: his entire organism was a machine for making mistakes.

His neighbours in his own line still caught the nimble penny as it passed, by their variety of resource: he spurned it, as one who would have none of their tricks. His only concession was in the labels; but he was too stupid even for these. He made them cry, " Oh, I say, look here ! " when prudence should have urged everybody to look the other way. He toiled over these effusions by night, submitted them, like so many Academy pictures, to his faithful partner as a hanging committee of one. His boldest—" Here to-day—Gone to-morrow: Now's your chance "—was a failure by the anti-climax of its relation to a Dutch oven with no interior parts. He was not without visitations of a flush of shame in regard to these devices; but he was able to lay the responsibility on the follies of the age.

There were attempts to help him by charitable ministrations, but he declined them all. The district visitors of his chapel urged a friendly composition with his creditors, and the almshouse as a haven of rest. He scouted the notion. He was to be helped as tradesmen are helped, by putting capital into his business, or not at all. That was the way to keep the flag flying. They gave him a dole: he repainted the signboard, and bought a new set of shirt collars, and of labels for the stock, both higher than ever. Then, as one awaiting developments, he looked up at the sky.

What he thought he saw there is easily stated

—the approving smile of the patriarch Job. The full meaning of that poem is that the hero will not take himself at the common valuation. He is not wicked; he is not a deserver of the judgments; he is only a sufferer for his Maker's good pleasure, and he accepts his doom. So, with this other one. He confessed to nothing unworthy of a shop-keeper; and, though he might endure the visita-tion, it was not for him to kiss the rod. He had been hit hard, but that was as it might be; he had not provoked the punishment by unrighteousness; and that was enough for him.

He failed to see that stupidity is the crime. The strokes were judgments after all, judgments for eyes that saw not, judgments for the failure to understand. Alack for the foolish folk of all the world who suffer so much more sharply than the wicked! They are never mentioned in the churches, yet all of us might unite in a form of common prayer on All Fools' Day for ease of their intolerable pangs.

They sold him up the other day; and, when last seen, he was a dazed inmate of "The Big House," watching a scheme of creation that had just warned him off the premises. The old wife, I have no doubt, surveyed their lost Eden from another wing of the building. Their very partner-ship of sorrow was dissolved. Pity the stupid, of your charity!

HEART FAILURES

I AM sometimes inclined to think that most of the failures among the little people are cases of heart failure—not of the organ, but of the soul within. This is particularly the case in the arts, where so much depends on the friendly visitation of nature. With most of us the will to win comes and goes like the changes in the cloud, and it is often strongest in those that have little to win with. All sorts of things bring on the corresponding alacrity to lose, and particularly the advance of years. People age all too quickly, I understand, as drapers or as haircutters, but this is nothing to the rate of decay in artists or writers. The very fineness of their sense of touch with the time renders them particularly subject to that disaster.

I knew one like this, who, without being at all a brilliant man, had maintained himself and his family for years as a fly of the hour in the newspapers and magazines. In his public character he was a thing of the gaudiest plumage and the most unforeseen eccentricities of flight; in his private capacity, a perfect ratepayer. In print he seemed to play pitch and toss with all the conventions of respectability. Out of it, he sat on vestries and broke his rest with the first croak of the baby in crises of whooping cough. A model husband and father, a model man, with quite a vein in mid-Victorian humour, and a genial optimism that left everyone the happier for his exertions.

Then came, in a night and a day, the swing round to paradox and pessimism, known in the trade, I believe, as the two p's, and he was left without a vocation. Hustling editors gave him to understand in a thousand ways, delicate or in-delicate, that he was a fogey. The spring fashions in ideas had changed, and he had not been suffi-ciently careful in watching the shop-windows of his rivals. New they were, whatever else they were not.

Think of how it must have fared with the older humour when Dickens appeared above the horizon, or with the older invective when Carlyle revealed himself to himself, quite as much as to others, in the " Sartor " ; " Our author," said an angry critic, " reminds us of the German pedant who was found jumping over the chairs and tables. When asked what he was doing, he replied that he was trying to be lively." This was a critic who could not see what was coming : Carlyle " caught on," though, no doubt, to the astonishment of the wholesale houses. Our author simply went on jumping and threw a whole school of prophecy out of work. Dreadful moment for his rivals when the very spirit of their age whispered " Too old," and when the most incurable of all diseases

G

stamped them with its mark in crows' feet of the brain.

Nor is this the worst of it. I suppose that certain families, like certain races, have their birthmark of some particular form of failure, and must be ever on their guard against the surprises of heredity. I knew of a family, of the old disappearing type, where most of the women had suffered generation by generation because most of the men had failed in grit. Not a few of the latter had been men of parts, but the crises of life had ever caught them at a disadvantage.

One of their best, whose career promised to turn the luck, told me that the knowledge of this infirmity had haunted him like a decree of fate. He was for ever feeling himself all over for the soft place. What agonies when the flesh seemed to give way, what rub, rub, rubbing, or other exercises in decision of character, for riddance of the spot that marked his doom. I lost sight of him, happily for my peace of mind, but I have often pictured him as failing in some supreme moment to hold some giddy height he had won, and falling headlong into the ruck of discomfiture to join the others of his name. There may be theme of great tragedy here.

My ratepayer tells me that he began life thinking he was going to fail in it. It was another note of the slackness of fibre in him—the kiss on the cheek of his beaten enemy, we remember, was the first. He had no sense of existence as a struggle; he dreamed of it as a thing that was all, more or less, an exchange of knightly offices—foolish child! He generally muddled matters, and could not conceive of himself as clever or anything of that sort. He thought it would be delightful just to live, doing nice things and getting your share of nice things done in return—exchanging good offices, in fact, as the Utopians of the story exchanged their washing.

Just to live—that was all he wanted, in the dear old Jacobean street, branching out of the dear old unreformed Strand, in which it was his happiness to spend his holidays. He was, in fact, a Jacobean of domestic architecture long before the revivalists of our day. The hopeless creatures of his early time were still in the mid-Victorian survival of mahogany sofas, tempered with horsehair, and of the passion for modernising old houses with the aid of stucco, wall-paper, and slabs of plate-glass. It was a mercy that the old street was spared. But he knew that it was beautiful, long before it occurred to him that he might possibly be a person of taste.

Many of us, no doubt, have a fair start in these beautiful intuitions, but too many throw it away. The old house was so beautiful, so quiet, so full of strange out-of-the-way corners. In one word, it was such a setting for the drama of the spirit, for its comedy in the garret play-room, for its tragedy

in the double tiers of subterraneans—the upper
for the great kitchen, the lower for coals and ghosts
—and for the other kinds in the general dignity
and comfort of the middle suites.

What hospitality in the great dining-table; in
the curtained four-poster, what intensity of repose!
With all this, sweet Thames running softly to the
view from the front—sometimes bearing a Lord
Mayor afloat on his way to Westminster—and a
flagged courtyard, shaded by most ancient trees,
in the rear. It was a house for wet days as for
bright days—in fact, for all the year round. On
the wet ones you burrowed deep in easy chairs and
read old books, all by yourself and undisturbed,
as a mere item of domestic concern. On the fine
days you went abroad to explore.

There, again, it was all fairyland. These were
the days before the Law Courts came to claim
broad acres for clearance, and especially a certain fragment of Carolinian London, no longer
to be matched within our boundaries. It was a
mystery of narrow, winding streets, of gables,
of overhanging storeys, from the upper windows
whereof, no doubt, neighbours shook hands without leaving their houses. When that went there
was still, for precious years, the solace of Holy-
well Street, Wych Street, and New Inn—one of
the oldest things of its kind in the capital.

From New Inn *The Spectator's* anonymous
" Batchelor " set forth every day, wigged, cocked-

hatted, and engaged in the nice conduct of a clouded cane, for Will's Coffee House and his daily encounter with Sir Roger de Coverley. The route march was by Drury Lane and Vinegar Yard, and so on to Russell Street, Covent Garden, now fallen on the evil times of the potato trade. The whole region was a sort of museum of the London of the past in its memorials of Roman and Saxon, Dane and Norman, one on the top of another. If you went deep enough with the spade you came on layers of the dead past, all perfectly sequent as from bottom to top, the latest nearest the surface, of course.

From New Inn it was but a stone's throw to Lyon's Inn. How place it now when everything is swept away? Enough to say that at Lyon's another stone might have broken a window of the Church of St. Mary le Strand, a going concern still, as it was when the charity children stood in the churchyard to sing hymns on the passage of Queen Anne to St. Paul's.

Lyon's, as the boy knew it, was mouldering to its ruin, and it had a fascination of terror for him as the refuge of shabby genteel crime. Here, in its vast paved courtyard, with grass sprouting between the cobbles, the forger, the begging letter writer, the cashiered army officer, the bogus company promoter, and now and again the man who united these industries, one or other, with murder, had their lodgings and their offices in one. Hither came Thurtell and his gang to lure their victim into the country ambush in which they butchered him as a new way of paying old gambling debts. Thackeray has preserved a fragment of the copy of verses sung under the gallows when they were strung up :—

His name was Mr. William Weare,
And he lived in Lyon's Inn.

. The boy had heard of these things, and they gave pause to his steps on the threshold of the wicked-looking old gateway—wicked as a place that might be expected to close with a snap on the wayfarer. The trap was evidently worked from the porter's lodge, where fiery eyes, glistening in the gloom above a dirty curtain of red baize, and a bottle-nose in the same key of colour, kept the gate by sheer moral force, and without any help from the arm of flesh.

On the rare occasions when these organs were not at their post of duty the boy rushed the opening of the trap, scoured the whole quadrangle at a run, and with another rush at the exit found safety again in the open street. In another stone's throw from the church he was on the home stretch by Strand Lane, a winding way still bearing quite visible traces of its origin as a cattle track to the river some twenty centuries ago. Here pausing for breath, he stared through battered railings into the Roman bath, Tudor in its latest attempt to bring itself up to date, where Legionaries had taken their morning plunge in the ice-cold spring, and after them Templars, home from the Holy Land, and then again generations of law students, to this day.

And then the Temple, not far off, or how could Templars come here for their morning dip? The ancient Inn of Court was beautiful in itself, beautiful in its sense of perfect peace. So near the roar of London, yet so far beyond the oppression of its reach, its hum but a sort of harmony of audible quiet, a mere indispensable background of silence, like the sound of bees. All was perfect— the old fountain, as yet unrestored, the old trees, their leaves light green against the sunlight, the birds, the flowers, the trim lawns, the great hall.

Here, especially, the boy felt that rare things had happened long ago, though he had yet to learn that one of them was the Elizabethan Bench and Bar, and, perhaps, the Queen herself attending a performance of *Twelfth Night*, Mr. Shakespeare's new play. The great garden, where the buds for the Wars of the Roses were most assuredly plucked in tradition, if in no other way—the cloisters, in extent but a glorified backyard, where the rank and fashion of London had once found the space all sufficing for their daily promenade— the very barber's shop in the corner, where the wigs, changeless in a world of change, are still on show, with last year's dead flies—all were so many properties of a play of dreamland for the urchin on his rounds.

Whatever else it was not, it was beautiful as a setting for holiday time. No doubt these ancient parts of ancient cities must go, if the cities are to keep their place in the van. Much of the central London of eld has gone, but how great the happiness of him who has known it in its perfection, who has passed his New Years' nights within sound of " The Bells of St. Clements," still there to ring-in those dawns of years to come, which are also the sunsets of years gone. The charm of London lies in that fine artistic blending of survivals with the latest growths, which gives one part of the city time to get old while the other is getting new.

At home once more the boy was still in a land where everything happened, and nothing was done. He lay coiled in the arm-chair, and read his classics of the adventurous life—Crusoe and Quixote, Robin Hood, Turpin and Sheppard, for at that age all is fish that comes into the net. The endless reading became a drug at last. The house was dreamland, as the streets had been : it was all a poesy of a past which was now going on for ever without change. The fire and candle of winter nights, the suns of summer afternoons and their luminous shadows, the river dotted with barge and steamer, oar and sail, were dreamland too.

It was so easy to live in that land of the holidays. When he tired of his bookish company he could find flesh and blood enough below stairs. The kitchen offered him a standing invitation, revering him as one whose knowledge of " print," whatever its import, was wisdom. " Such a reader, and knew everything," except when he knew just nothing at all, and then he was best fun. He was deep in the lore of the broadside ballads, still coming out as the latest garlands of song when Queen Victoria was young, and now things of price for their rarity.

He was asked to sing the ballads, with a promise of goodies at will for his fee. He hung his head. What was the matter with him? The head still lay low. Was he shy? Now it was nodded. That was easily managed; he should sing in " the basket "—a receptacle for table linen waiting for the wash. Another nod, and he was lifted into the basket bodily and the lid replaced, the crevices serving as inlets for air, and outlets for melody. He had now only to keep his face to the wall to escape the public gaze.

Those who gave the goodies had a right to call the tune; and as " Meet Me by Moonlight " was a great favourite, that was generally their choice. From this safe retreat he piped his roundelay, but slightly disturbed by the tittering which he, at least, could not see. The basket thus became tuneful as some contrivance of an Egyptian rite, and in the unearthly fashion of a sound that was a voice and nothing more.

> Daylight may do for the gay,
>> For the thoughtless, the heartless, the free;
> But there's something about the moon's ray
>> That is sweeter for you and for me.

I offer no defence of this effusion; it is enough to say that such things were sung with conviction in the spacious times of great Victoria.

What wonder such a boy promised to become one of the worst cases of heart failure known to the books. The ratepayer has often told me that, at this stage of his existence, he had no hope of ever being clever enough to earn his living. To be fair, he had not the slightest inclination to begin. On the rare occasions on which he stooped to meditation on a career, he thought he would go on wandering among the old streets and the old houses, and make a modest income by playing the flute in the Inns of Court.

A SORT OF A SINKING

THIS mood of heart failure is very natural: the wonder is how any of the weaker sort of Little People contrive to escape a sense of depression as haunting as a Satanic whisper. The meaner can hardly need a second temptation, when the issue is so clearly foreseen. How struggle against the world forces and their inevitable mastery? What is a poor me to do? It is such a big, " haughty " sort of world, and I am such a nobody in it.

Underlying all the brag of the incompetent, all their whistling to keep up their courage in the dark, is this feeling of the immensity of the odds against them—" all Lombard Street to a China orange." The wealth, the power, the pride of station, the pride of birth, the confidence induced by the suit of Sunday clothes for every day in the week, and by the certainty of the day's dinner in perpetuity—this, on the one side; and, on the other, only a poor chap. Then " happy low lie down," be thankful for small mercies, keep a civil tongue in your head, and when in doubt touch your cap.

Most of the hurrying millions of the street have this for their sole idea of the tactics of battle. It does not preclude the sense of revolt, but it keeps that in its place. Swear if you will, but swear in waste places or up the chimney, and so keep the matter between you and the stars.

Above all, there is the certainty that you must expect no valid help from your mates. You are all a flock of sheep, and a single bark of the collie is more than a match for your collective bleat. You know that, if it comes to business, every mutton of you will have to face him without a backer. The hornless brows may duck for a moment, but in a moment more it will be a riot of flying scuts. Even now, as he leaps on the mass of wedged fleeces, every sheep's head of you feels that it will be one to one in the last resort.

Call you this a backing o' your friends? Well, it is but such as you will get. The ratepayer has often told me of his horror of petty people, that is to say, though he hardly knows it, his mistrust of his own kind. He abhors their society, their all pervading suggestion of futility, their limitation of outlook, their dull and spiritless talk. It gives him a sort of a sinking, he is pleased to say. They may keep each other in countenance while the glass goes round, and the policeman is not in the way, but for cohesion they are as parched sand. They would leave you in the lurch in a moment, turn king's evidence against you at need, collar you from behind, while the strong arm operated from the other side.

This disposition to make terms with your destiny lies at the root of our national snobbishness. Never shall I forget a figure that I encountered the other day in one of the cemeteries. There was something in his proceedings which did not suggest the affliction of a personal loss. He seemed as one trying to give himself an air of consequence, by striking an attitude of bereavement before the most expensive graves.

At first all my sympathy went out to him as I saw him in a pose of the most poignant sorrow before the tomb of a deceased Baron of the Exchequer. His head was bowed as in resignation, he had a handkerchief in his grasp. I passed by on the other side, as a matter of simple good feeling, and so did the others who happened to be in the way. All reverently averted their gaze, and, in some instances, other handkerchiefs came forth.

'Twas all very well, but presently, in a neighbouring avenue, I found him in a similar state of dejection before a costly monument to the virtues of a deceased Grand Cross of the Bath. Even then it was possible to give him the benefit of the doubt, with the reflection that his whole family had perhaps devoted their lives to the service of the State. But, beyond this, charity itself refused to go when I found him once more engaged in the same manner in front of the very latest addition to the collection of titled dust. It was evidently his notion of a blameless holiday in places of public resort.

This time, I think, he recognised me as one who had seen him at the other tombs, for he conquered his sorrow in an instant and hurried off. It was only his way of bragging the acquaintance of his betters without the risk of a cut.

My old friend the Oracle, again, is a snob of the workhouses. He looks down on a busy scene which he has long quitted, from a bow window of a palatial establishment for the poor, in one of our chief thoroughfares. He is the leader of the common room there, and he rules it with a rod of iron by virtue of his disdain for the other inmates. He snubs them to death for their *ignerance*—so it pleases him to sound it, on authority, no doubt, for he has authority for everything.

As they read their morning paper they come to him for points of the speeches, and for the difficult words. I once saw a whole ward of such lame dogs waiting for his help over a stile, in the shape of the name of that King of Babylon who went to grass for his sins, and whose story, no doubt, is but the myth of the first introduction of asparagus. " Neb—Neb—Neb ! " stammered the reader, giving it up at last to mop a heated brow. "Ask Him ! " cried the others in chorus. The Oracle vouchsafed a " Nebuchadanzer," without a moment's hesitation; and the reading went on.

Nothing is too hard for him. He has read Moore's Almanac for the past sixty years, and he has all its memorabilia and all its curious lore by heart. He can tell you off-hand when the potato was introduced into England, the year and the day on which umbrellas first appeared in our public thoroughfares, the best way of removing grease spots from silk, the characters of Charles the Second, Oliver Cromwell, and Bamfylde Moore Carew, King of the Beggars; the whole story of the murder in the Red Barn.

With this he is a perfect Jack Cade of pauper revolt. He has made the rules of the institution the study of his days and nights, and he can stand up to the master on the question of Yorkshire pudding as a logical accompaniment of roast beef. He has always been credited with the secret authorship of a letter to the papers, years ago, which exposed the management to a storm of obloquy, and led to a question in Parliament, and almost to a public inquiry. He has never avowed as much, but the mere suspicion of it is a power in reserve. His nod is a certificate of social standing for the new inmates. He questions them closely as to their antecedents, and, according to the result, gives or withholds the notice which determines their place in the community. In one word, his horror of petty people, though it may have begun with a sense of his own significance, is now, in itself, a mastery of a kind.

People like this yield basely to their lot of littleness; there are others who yield with a grace of submission that makes a worse case, if you like, but that still has a pathos of its own. They repay the trouble of a glance, for, in our day of social revolt, they are a vanishing race, with their full acceptance of the law of caste. They and theirs, so far as they care to look into the future, are for ever doomed to subservience. They stand on a lower range of the pyramid of better and worse that has swells for its apex and poor coves for its base. They know their duty, and they exact as much deference from their inferiors as they yield to those above.

I have known one such, and I venerate him as the last of a race, as I venerated in my childhood the Aztecs in the show. He is an artisan, and his whole nature is subdued to the circumstances of his lot. With him society as it stands is a fact of nature—a fact and a force; and he worships it as his progenitor of the prime worshipped sun and storm.

Here be thunder, lightning, earthquake, heat and cold—let us lie low! My friend sees the same necessity in the phenomena of his day, and humbles himself in the same manner. Here are the sack, the hungry belly, the all-powerful bloke that rides in his carriage, and could buy up a thousand "such as me"; let us touch our caps! The worst of hardships is to be too poor to afford the luxury of making an enemy. He saves with the most desperate assiduity; he works overtime; his week-end is the park, because it is only a penny ride; his annual holiday a twopenny ride, tempered with the waxwork show. The latter is his encyclopædic epitome of the world of sense, with its clustered courts of Europe at one end of the scale, and its gallows-tree at the other, both mainly as rewards for " them as don't behave theirselves," with a difference of result, as between " them as don't get found out and them as do."

All he knows is that he must work hard, and put by as he can, for all the haps of life, chancing the odds for the rest. It is a slow business. There is the boy's club-foot, and what are you going to make of him with education so dear? The girl's typewriting and shorthand may be a career, " but there's five hundred in the school, and all but fifty of 'em right above her 'ead." And then the rest of the brood, and, above all, the dear mother hen! Well, " fight on, my merry men all," put by, put by: £67 3s. 4d. in the bank —" if you don't believe me there's the book to prove it—and both of us as good as ever if it wasn't for the wife's sciatiker. Oh, crool! can't sleep o' nights; and my rick in the back; you know what I told yer of—when I made a fool o' myself with that 'eavy weight."

The wife's case is one of still more perfect submission to the overmastering powers. Surely

H

the virtues of prudence can no further go; no, not in the lives of champion anchorites and saints. It is not only the washing *for* the family, but the washing *of* it, for its morning turn-out, " clean 'ands and face, and clean collars—must send 'em respectable to school." The feeding of them involves the nicest compromise between the claims of frugality and those of nutrition—cereals mainly for the children, and a bit extra in meat for the man, because he is the bread-winner and must keep up his strength. For herself, apparently, anything that they don't happen to want will serve.

It is a life as exasperating as that of the great man who was without one redeeming vice. The master goes out at half-past five to his work; she rises earlier still to give him a hot breakfast before he starts. " No use my tellin' 'er I won't have it; I can't tie 'er down to 'er bed." The first to turn out and the last to turn in are things that often go together. And, besides the whole work of the house, there is also the bit of dress-making—corresponding to the husband's odd jobs after hours—as a means of increasing the hoard at the bank.

In this part of their labours both of them show their incurable, their invincible fitness for their lot as little people. Their charges are for nothing but their working time, at the lowest rates of the market. With this and the exact cost of material as certified by voucher, you have the bill. Such people have absolutely no sense of buying in the cheapest market and selling in the dearest—in short, of doing as they are done by all their lives.

It is a curious case, and I watch it with the greatest interest to see how it is going to turn out, sometimes with misgiving, I am fain to admit. The thought of " anything happening " to either of them—as things do sometimes happen, we are bound to admit—is quite disheartening. I have had the same feeling sometimes in watching a bird at work in a nest, with its attendant possibilities of mischance in the shape of a thunderstorm, or of a boy prospecting for a chaplet of eggs. I have even hinted as much to him in the warning, " Take care of your health." He is ready for that: " What about my sick club ? "

It were bad manners to carry it further, yet no one can deprive me of my thoughts. I have visions of children weeping for their Rachel, or for her mate, lying still under the white sheet; and of a whole scheme of earthly providence wrecked in a twinkling, and life to be faced anew in all its hideous realities with £67 3s. 4d. in the bank.

It is no fancied danger, and I happen to know that, in rare moments of depression, he, on his part, sometimes regards it with " a sort of a sinking." Every day she sends him forth—and both know it, without breathing a word—to the chances of the lofty scaffold and the slipping plank; every day he leaves her with the same sort of well-bred silence, to the only less sensational risks of her own toil. It is a model case. With this as a highest possible of the score of virtue, how few can ever care to aim at the mark !

OUR BETTERS

ALL this makes for reverence for betters, and the country-side is the place for that. Little rustic people still touch their caps, though too often only with a jerk of the thumb. The survival is better than nothing : it is at least a recognition of the fact that the Hall—and be hanged to it !—can hit hard when it likes. So the cottage stands for a submission which is needs must—if only where the devil drives. Between the two there are the villas that bear a sort of feudal relationship to the great house by keeping a few dependents in their place, as the Hall keeps their masters. The villas send deputies once a week to the Hall, to render an account of their stewardship of subservience as it concerns cook, housemaid, gardener, and page-boy, and generally speaking to do homage at afternoon tea.

The whole life of the settlement still lies in the hollow of the feudal hand. The old lordship of the manor still holds, though by an agency more potent than the sword. It is trade now as the source of power, where it was once war. Our last of the barons, to date, was in hides, and amassed a colossal fortune. Then, looking out for a haven and the joys of power for the evening of his days, he came down here and bought the great house as the centre of things, and all the region round about—within at least a bow-shot of the longest range.

With the estate went all the life upon it, man and beast and bird in the air, as effectually as if they had been scheduled to him in an appendix of the deed. For, by the one decisive stroke of the pen, he acquired ownership of their habitations, their means of comfort, and their means of life. Try to draw a breath here, except on the highway, without his leave or his relict's,—nay, I will go further : try to get born here ! The mere incident of nativity may take place anywhere : a drab may increase our population by an accident at the roadside; but anything like permanent settlement is quite out of the question. It is " welcome, little stranger " to ditch or cottage, and then " out you go " as soon as you are able to fend for yourself. You can never hope to marry and settle here, and have children in your turn.

The Hall simply keeps the cubic content of house-room quite stationary, and so teaches all surplus population to know its place—which is the London slum. A new cottage is an extraordinary event—a cottage reared on what has hitherto been virgin soil, and extending the village bounds into the wilderness of verdure. You may foretell to a dozen or so the count of inhabitants, year by year, nay, century by century. We are just enough for

the needs of the estate in digging, ploughing, sow-
ing, small shop-keeping, and what not; and there
we stop, without fail, at the bare sufficiency for use
and ornament.

Ornament counts : our peasantry in one of their
attributes are a part of the view, like the cows and
the sheep, and without them the house parties
might miss something when they come down.
The neat cottage, clean-pinafored children going
to school, sun-bonneted mothers hanging out the
clothes, belong as much to the effect of the look
of the thing as the great rose garden and the
fairy dell. It is all beautiful, beyond doubt, restful, and everything else that makes for the sense
of the happy land.

The lady of the manor holds us all in silken
thrall, the poor by her doles, the other sort by her
hospitality. We are an epitome, as I have said,
the whole body politic in a nutshell. Our better
sort are in the roomier houses, half cottage, half
mansion, the note whereof is a jobbing gardener,
and a man to look after the trap, or even the carriage, and to wait at table.

Try to beat this system if you can as a scheme
for the eternal duration of things. The retired
civil servant is hard by, in the old house with
the show staircase, its oak black as ebony with
age and shining as the faces of the elect.
The place has been going on for centuries like
that, always with such people in it, or their social

equivalents of the time. Can it ever pass away? The retired civil servant takes a fatherly interest in all the charities. Once a year he conducts the whole mothers' meeting to the Crystal Palace at an incredible cost of time and patience, not to say of hard cash, all cheerfully borne. He sub-ruled an Indian province in his day, and, on occasion, bearded its dusky princes in their state. The retired clergyman keeps him in countenance.

Oh, the ineffable peace of it all! It would be stagnation but for the womankind: thanks to this sex, with its quickness, its sense of being, its sharp contrasts of taste, temperament, and temper, you have always a pulse of life. We move— under the microscope. The clergyman's daughters drive to the meet; the barrister's wife thinks they might sometimes be better employed; the civil servant's wife moots the question of what are we going to do about the wife of the drug merchant, still in trade, who has just made a lodgment in our midst. He does something wholesale—it is rumoured in a slum—and drives every morning to catch the early train. There are darker rumours of his having once sold pills over a counter. But his wife, though needy before her marriage, was of the county in her place of origin, and is indubitably " nice." Our afternoon teas hum with the sense of momentous decisions, and the hum is life.

The woman who is hanging out the clothes accepts all this as mastery, and not the woman only, but her partner. It is a mass of convergent forces—political, religious, social, personal—that put resistance out of the question. He can't make it better, and it might be so very much worse. He works at the Hall as under-man to the under-gardener, at wages that keep him quite close to the margin of subsistence; and he knows that the slightest mistake would send him, and his, roofless to the high road with his " sticks " in charge. As well square up to his Maker as try conclusions with the earthly power that holds him in thrall. He is the automaton of a round of duties, fixed, invariable, and in their lulling sense of use and wont almost precluding the sense of hardship.

In early morning he fares afield to his appointed task; but before starting he stops to cut the household fuel for the day from the fallen boughs. He has a sort of right to rotten branches for his own fire, feudal no less by what it gives than by what it withholds. You are aware of him, as you watch from your windows, by flash and report in the usual order of sequence—the shine of the axe in the morning light, and its thud in the tree stump used as a chopping-block. Then, after scattering a few handfuls of corn for the chickens, he lights his pipe, and is soon lost in the greenwood and the morning mist.

His face is quite inscrutable for complaint,
though not exactly for little ease. It is hard lined
with endurance rather than purpose, fixed as in the
setting of submission to a lot. " Lifers " in prison
have sometimes the same look. They know the
rules and avoid the penalties: nothing is going
to happen against them, and nothing for them but
food, shelter, and bondman's work to the end.
They have attained, in their rude way, to the void
of all desire.

The human powers that shape and rule are
as much above the peasant as the elemental forces
of which they really form a part. He neither
loves nor hates them : he accepts, with the Eastern
formula " I hear and I obey." They expect him
to behave himself according to his station, and to
renew his pact every Sunday at the hour of public
prayer. One attendance at church will do; but,
as part of its obligations, his croak must contribute
to the discord of the hymn and his *Amen* must
ring true.

This is the parson's doing, in his quality of
the one who has the right to expect. He usually
differs wholly from his brother in town by virtue
of his sense of mastery of the situation. He im-
poses conditions with the full certainty of his
power to enforce. He has not to hold the candle
to the devil, by humouring or cajoling his people
to fill his church. There is no necessity of that
kind in his parish, no " Hail, fellow; well met ! "

to the tippling loafer, nor laying on of clean hands in compulsory caresses of soiled babies encountered in his rounds. He can afford to be a beneficent tyrant, austere and distant, like the Corsair of the Byronic ideal; it is his trick of governance, and he exacts the same awe from his flock as he offers to the higher powers.

Why not, since virtue is nobility in the highest, and, by his calling, he is of the noble order? It is not for him to play down to the lapsed masses: leave such condescensions to popular bishops who have been known to tuck up their cassocks for foot races with the riff-raff of the slums. His high Anglicanism is theocracy in the saddle: there will be time enough to sink to the arts of persuasion when he has lost the power to command. Temperament prompts that way; he may be hard as nails, cold as ice, an abstraction unloving and unloved, like a Commissioner of Excise. This, of course, is true only of certain natures, and it does not preclude an occasional Dr. Primrose in a rural cure.

The Wakefield type tends to become extinct in our day of rigidly defined priestly claims. The new model is a poor provision of spiritual unction for the chambers of the sick: I have heard of calls to repentance, and official assurances of final hope, scarcely more impressive in tone and quality of utterance than a deliverance of the gramophone. The country people have a phrase for such ministrations—" 'Twas a cold death-bed."

Thus everything in the village makes for the sense of lordship by appointed rulers, civil and religious, and in its nature is still perfect feudality tempered by the forms of modern life. It is never more marked than when the working girls are brought down for a week-end visit to the great house. The visitors are lodged suitably in the cottages, and have their attention at once directed to the green pastures, in which they are expected to delight as in something never seen before.

Then, in due course of park and stables and links and lawn, comes the crowning mercy of the Hall. Here they have a glimpse of the paradise of the state apartments, still in brown holland, but not unwilling to doff it from arm or leg of a chair to gratify vulgar curiosity as to the glories beneath. The next step is inevitable, though it is not in the programme: they plead for a sight of the bedroom and dressing-room of their hostess, as neophytes who would fain fathom the mysteries of Venus armed. Their custodian, the housemaid, rather sharp and snubby with them, as being of their own class, yields to importunity, and they enter in.

It is well meant, beyond all question, but is it altogether wise? Where is fancy—in Socialism —bred? As often as not perhaps in this too rich display of down and silken hangings, triple pile for the tread, toilet batteries, massed for deadly execution, where the meanest thing is of shell or precious metal, the richest of gemmed gold, where all imaginable luxury, in fact, contrasts with all imaginable privation in the homes to which the visitors are so soon to return.

Now in town, though we are still ruled by our betters, it is in quite another way : they respect the forms of independence. Never shall I forget my first membership of a political society. It was called a Liberal and Radical Defence Association, and I had joined it from a sense of duty to my country, and to a minute division of a metropolitan borough in which I then happened to reside. We were seventeen. The world—I had almost said the universe—thought there were more of us, but this was our exact count : I know it, for I held high office in the group. We had quite recently been called into corporate being by a local resident of distinction who aspired to a seat in Parliament in the Radical interest, and whose house was in one of our most self-respecting squares.

I had been drawn to him because he was evidently a perfect ratepayer. I knew little of him at the time, but I afterwards learned that he was a man of many societies, by preference of those with an easy condition of membership. He wrote many capital letters after his name, and wrote them as often as he could. Some few, however, implied a real qualification : he had made his modest fortune as the proprietor of a highly successful boarding school in a salubrious part of the coast. It was run on the time-honoured principle of the division of labour : grey-haired drudges in his service supplied the scholarship; he was solely responsible for the circulars. The parents thought he knew everything, and sometimes sent kindly messages to him from their death-beds. He wore a white tie to the last.

In his new venture he had made most of us subservient to his patriotic purposes by employing us in his domestic concerns. Some mended his boots, his coats, or his chairs and tables; one cleaned his windows, another was the father of his parlourmaid; and one more, a marine store dealer, bought the rags, bones, and bottles from his kitchen.

Others were attached to him by similar ties of self-interest, and, as their patron as well as friend, he had gradually indoctrinated them with the purest principles of the old Liberal creed. They had first formed a mere Liberal Association, but he had induced them to adopt the second part of their title, in breathless haste, in consequence of an unexpected Radical victory at a bye-election. They were supposed to pay a modest subscription of a shilling a year, but he was by no means exigent in the matter of arrears.

It is enough to say that the money was always there for all our needs. The meetings were held in his drawing-room, and single knocks at the door announced a presence on his threshold. There was a further announcement of a kind in the strident energy with which newcomers wiped their boots on the mat. The servant awed them all, including her own parent, with the severity of her air and the immaculate neatness of her evening uniform of black and white. Their host attracted them by his heartiness of welcome; his wife kept them in their place by a certain loftiness of manner acquired by her management of mothers' meetings; his secretary—another lady—was in the note of authority tempered by good fellowship. The treasurer, a twin influential resident, called him " Jack."

The last-named persons formed our aristocratic and ruling element, and they were but four in all. The others—modesty compels me to leave myself out of the reckoning—were our not too fierce democracy, for but one had anything in him of the spirit of revolt. This one was the Ragman. He, too, was influential in his way, for his aid promised to be invaluable in the storm and stress of the General Election that was close at hand. He was a master of the arts of appeal, and especially that of " billing " the neighbourhood. He had acquired this in the course of business, for he lived by advertising's artful aid. His shop windows were covered with posters of the most appealing nature, constantly varying in form to meet the defections of public interest : " Now's your time to turn rags, bones, bottles into gold! We defy competition! Highest prices in the trade."

But his letterpress was nothing to his illustrations. His colours were all primitives, and raw at that, and he knew exactly how to compel the passer-by to halt and read. He luxuriated in representations of sudden transitions from poverty to wealth, all owing to the happy thought of doing business with him.

Cooks docile to these suggestions were seen driving away in their carriages as a result of their own foresight and of his reckless liberality. He had but to transfer the wisdom thus acquired to our service in the crisis of party conflict to become simply indispensable. We could not do without him. He knew all the best bill-posting stations in the neighbourhood; he was able to show us that one single cartoon at the corner " hit the traffic in the eye "—these were his words—better than two at that. He was a perfect scholar in dead walls; and, if he could see no farther through them than anybody else, he was quite illuminatingly aware of all the possibilities of their surface.

He was now ready to devote his entire frontage to our service for the stress of battle. His appeals to the cook and the scullion were to disappear for the moment, to make way for political caricatures in the interest of our cause. These, as we saw them in proof, were as rich in colouring as his other masterpieces : " Here's a Chance to Send an Honest Man to Westminster," and " What Price the Tories Now ? "   His personages still drove in chariots, but this time as " Bloodsuckers " gorged with the plunder of the community.   And sometimes, in more daring flights, he vilified them in scathing verse.   At times, too, he lent his vans to our orators, and took the chair on his own tail-boards.

He had but one weakness, and that really was a virtue under another name : as a fierce democrat, he began to resent the supremacy of our founder. At committee meetings he was the only man of our rank and file who did not sit on the edge of his chair.   He made a point of leaning against the back of it, and of adopting a critical attitude in regard to the introductory address.   We trembled ; but now and then we applauded—when we got outside.   He asked questions, he took objections on points of order ; and it was impossible to smile him down.   The harassed administration at last made him Inspector of Publicity, and this for a time restored unanimity to our deliberations.

It was desirable, for we had ever so much to do.   It was not merely to watch home politics : we had to extend our vigilance to the affairs of Europe and of the world at large.   Our founder seemed to survey all human concerns every morning for opportunities of " catching on," and he occasionally summoned us, at a moment's notice, with a three-lined whip which it was not easy to withstand.

On one occasion, for instance, we were impelled to address a serious remonstrance to the ruler of Russia on the subject of his treatment of the Poles. It was passed without a dissentient voice, though I can hardly say at a full meeting. The cobbler was busy; the carpenter was not very well; there were other abstentions, and we mustered but nine, all told. That, however, was our own secret; and the resolution went forth as the voice of the association.

It was proposed by the Ragman, who had previously been consulted as to its terms, and who had made significant reserves as to the omission of the word "autonomy," of which he secretly asked me the exact meaning. It was seconded by the father of the parlourmaid, and carried without a dissentient voice. Our founder then moved that one copy of it should immediately be forwarded to the Russian Ambassador; another to the Premier of the Government ·in being; and a third to the office of the local paper devoted to our cause. The instruction was duly entered on the minutes, and we had tea.

It was a memorable evening, and it was but one of many of the same sort. Our voice went forth from time to time to instruct the Sultan in the government of his European provinces, and to the Republic of the United States in regard to a more equitable treatment of its coloured population. The resolutions were sometimes officially acknowledged by the parties concerned, and all this gave dignity to our agenda paper, and interest to our work.

We lived very happily for awhile, but life was not to glide on like this for ever. The penalty of being one of the betters of the little people is that they are apt to resent your superiority, while they obey your lead. Perhaps if we had been capable of a more charitable judgment of our wire-puller, we should have seen that he was one of the smallest of us all. We voted as one man while we were on the edges of his chairs, but we seemed to lapse into faction as soon as we slipped off and gained the street.

The movement was led by the Ragman. He had been mollified, but not altogether appeased. In the first place, he was hurt by not being allowed to sign the resolution to the Muscovite ruler, in his quality of an office holder of our association. In the next, he had not been treated properly, or he chose to think so, at our conversazione. He had offered to nominate a " caterer " for refreshments who would " do us prime," and to recite The Charge of the Light Brigade. The latter proposition was enthusiastically accepted, the former declined on the ground that the matter had already been the subject of correspondence with another candidate. He chose to sneer at this in a manner that some of us thought uncalled for, and to affect to scent a job. The recitation was a success, but his want of cordiality throughout the general course of the evening cast a gloom over the entertainment.

We all hoped it would blow over, but we were cruelly undeceived at our next meeting, when a letter was read in which he resigned his office as Inspector of Publicity, and implicitly, of course, resumed his entire freedom of action. It was acknowledged with expressions of regret, which, however, he was not there to receive in person, and we saw nothing of him till our first annual meeting.

This was devoted, of course, to a survey of the year's work, and to the presentation of the financial report and balance sheet. He made no objection to this instrument while it was under discussion, if discussion it could be called. We were agreeably surprised to find that our treasurer still held a balance of eight pounds seven and fourpence to the credit of our account. It was a masterpiece of good husbandry, I could but think, considering how little we had contributed to the result. The Ragman, however, punctuated this part of the report with ominous "Hums!" and "Ha's!" and sniffs, and with a portentous "That's all, is it?" as we were about to pass the usual vote of thanks. He left before we came to the vote, and I made a hasty excuse for following him and having it out.

"A very satisfactory meeting," I said, as I overtook him in the street.

" Hum ! "

" And a good sum to our credit."

" Ha ! "

" I had no idea we had so much in hand."

" No more had nobody else : they've owned it at last."

" I don't exactly follow you—owned what ? "

" That they've got some of our coin in their pockets. See what I mean ? "

" Of course they have; but what of that ? "

" What did I tell yer ? "

" I don't know that you ever told me anything; but suppose you did."

" Well, yer see; they say so theirselves."

" Of course they do; it's the balance sheet."

With that there came into my mind the horrid suspicion that this was perhaps the first balance sheet the Ragman had ever encountered in his life. I determined to put it to the test.

" Do you happen to know what a balance sheet is ? "

" Not me," he said cheerfully.

It was but too clear : he evidently regarded the whole thing as a confession of embezzlement extorted by its author's fears.

" I thought something was going on," he continued. "Twelve and six for refreshments for that conversationy: my missis would have done it for half a sov."

"Cheap enough as it stands, I think."

"Six bob of it for cake. I didn't touch a mossel myself. 'Ow much did you—?"

"I really don't remember."

"Funny, ain't it?"

"Why, surely you don't mean to insinuate—?"

"Not me; but there it is in black and white, and in their own words."

"Well; so it ought to be."

"That's jest what I say; but they've bin a long time about it."

"Nothing of the sort. Don't you understand the nature of a balance sheet? It's part of the report."

"*I* never knowed nothing about it; did you?"

"Of course not."

"There y'are! Seems they've 'ad it all the time."

"Had what? Out with it!"

"Our 'a'pence."

"Why not?"

"Then why didn't they say so, eh? Couldn't put it off no longer; that's how it looks to me."

"I wish you good-night!"

I left him in disgust. It was evident that, in his highly original view of it, a balance sheet was a kind of sheet of penitence in which defaulters atoned for their crimes. In this view our respected founder, oppressed by the sense of his own defalcations, had finally blurted out the truth, and stood, so to speak, at our bar awaiting judgment.

I don't know what happened after that, but I know what did not. My friend never got into Parliament. Our meetings steadily declined, till they reached the vanishing point below the quorum, and the association was dissolved. Its founder, however, subsequently had an easy fall on the gown of an alderman of the County Council.

LITTLE PEOPLE IN LOVE

THE Ratepayer has often told me of another interesting figure of his early days, who, but for him, might have been too timid for the greatest of all ventures—love. He was a loutish fellow verging on thirty, and an odd jobber of the house in which the boy passed his holidays. He afterwards went into the Life Guards. Nigh forty years after their meeting my friend came upon strange traces of their acquaintance in a tattered portfolio of manuscript yellow with age. The big one had great strength and as much simplicity and good nature; their friendship began by little mock contests between them at wrestling and fisticuffs, in which, somehow, the boy always contrived to get the upper hand.

This was perhaps due in part to other than purely physical causes on the part of Nobble—James Nobble, as he was named. He was confessedly " no scholar," and, in the stress of conflict, the sense of intellectual inferiority may have unnerved his arm. Though the smaller combatant was still but a dot of twelve, callow, and with a curly head, he imposed on his antagonist as a giant of learning by showing him his school-books and his certificates, and prating to him in a language which it pleased both to call French. Now this was a heavy handicap against poor Nobble, who came before the time of Board Schools, and who, at a very early age, had been sent out to help his mother keep house for the two. He admired everything the boy did in the scholastic way, and most of all his ornamental writing.

The teaching of this wholly superfluous art was one of the most reprehensible practices of the academy in which the boy was brought up. It impressed the parents, and that was its sufficient justification from the proprietary point of view. Once a year the lads brought home with them a portentous sheet of cardboard emblazoned with all the skill of the illuminator, and bearing commemorative reference to some historical event.

On one occasion, for instance, the inscription informed the reader and his remotest posterity that " The Battle of Trafalgar " was " Fought on the 21st October, 1805—between the Combined Fleets of France and Spain, and England—The former Commanded by Admirals Villeneuve and Gravina —And the latter by Admiral Lord Nelson, who was Killed in the Moment of Victory." The last line was canopied by a mass of flourishes, designed as a conventional representation of clouds of glory, while brilliant variations of the same kind gave the whole thing the note of patriotic pride. "Admiral Lord Nelson " was in old English, "Admirals Villeneuve and Gravina " in an inferior script, and the entire composition was kept together by little birds in flourishes, with dots for their eyes.

This masterpiece of craftsmanship may be said to have finished off Nobble, and kept him for ever in bonds to the boy. The poor fellow did not know that nearly every bit of it had been done by a drudge of an usher in his capacity of writing master. How could he? The boy was hardly aware of it himself. He had pencilled it out in his crude way, and the master had merely corrected it in ink for the finished copy. By labours of this sort every pupil in the school was enabled, without conscious deception, to pose as the Crichton of his time.

In this state of affairs it happened that Nobble had one day to confess to his superior that he was in love. His Thisbe was a housemaid who served on the other side of the party wall, and much had happened between them in glances of admiration and encouragement, in spite of that obstacle, or perhaps because of it. The moment had now come for a declaration, which Nobble was firmly persuaded required the formality of a letter. But how write the letter, since he was so totally deficient in all the arts?—how read one, in fact, if he should receive an answer?

In this dilemma he bethought himself of the adept in ornamental writing, and, breathing his tender secret to that artist, offered him a fee of twopence for his secretarial labours. The boy listened with the most perfect gravity, and undertook to give his assistance both in composition and penmanship. He would have spurned the fee, but his pocket money was running low, and, besides, he was already a little beyond that age of innocence in which he had gone after wildfowl in the courtyard of Somerset House.

The pair were soon closeted in the shed in which the lover cleaned the boots, and the scribe prepared to take instructions from the client by asking him what he wanted to say. This, however, though regular, was hardly the right method in the extremely peculiar circumstances of the case. Nobble simply scratched his head, and said he didn't know, at the same time delicately hinting that his being gravelled for lack of matter was the very reason why he had sought professional assistance. He was equally ignorant of the lady's Christian name or surname, but he had hopes that the letter might begin " Dear Miss," and might be thrown over the wall the next time she came out to dust the mats. His adviser made a note of this and other instructions; and, after a few more questions—one touching the date of a possible interview—he withdrew to write the letter out of his own head.

His first care was to rule his note-paper so as to make it look more like an exercise book, and then, after several failures due to his desire to attain perfection both in script and style—one of them an attempt to introduce a few birds in flourishes—he achieved the following :—

" DEAR MISS,—I write to inform you that my name is Nobble, and that I should be pleased to take you to a music hall any evening it may suit. There is a very nice entertainment at the Middlesex, but I leave that to you. Dear Miss, I don't remember that I was ever so fond of anybody as I am of you. You seem to have such nice eyes and hair, likewise such a nice way of walking about. I thought so the very first time I saw you. So conclude with my respectful compliments, and for the honour of your name.—Yours most obediently,

"ABELARD."

The boy had warmed to his task, as he had realised that what had hitherto been a hated exercise in *belles-lettres* or other branches, now meant professional income. There was something more : young as he was, he was excessively precocious ; and he had often wondered what it might be like to fall in love, and to have to conduct oneself accordingly.

At the same time, such are the inconsistencies of our nature, he thought Nobble a donkey for letting himself get into such a state. This, however, by the way : he had done his best. The composition was written in his best writing prize manner, the t's rising but half way towards the skies, the l's and h's almost touching the blest abodes. It had been hard work, and there were moments when his tongue protruded considerably from his mouth with the effort of concentration, and even curled up at the tip. He assured his employer, however, that it was far from being his very best, and Nobble, to whom all degrees of merit in this line were necessarily unknown, easily took him at his word.

The lover held the letter out at arm's length, and, evidently reserving his final judgment, said that he liked the look of it at a first glance. He then entered on the labours of analysis by asking the meaning of certain crosses at the bottom of the page. Our author informed him that they were kisses.

A debate arose on this point, Nobble's finer taste hazarding the opinion that this looked too free at the start. They were struck out by desire, and then the employer, perhaps secretly tormented by the apprehension of a certain want of ardour in the body of the work, timidly suggested the substitution of " it would do me proud " to take you to a music hall, instead of " I should be pleased." The boy assured him that no such locution was to be found in the select compositions of the English essayists which was the text-book of his school. Nobble, however, with a sense of the tremendous issues at stake, insisted on having his way on this point, and the draft was amended accordingly.

He next wanted to know, with all imaginable respect for superior attainments, why he was called Nobble at the opening of the letter and Abelard at the close. His expert assured him that this was in accordance with the best practice of the best models. They almost invariably took a pseudonym, the more tender the better; and the one chosen in this instance was the name of the most famous writer of love letters that ever lived. There could be no ambiguity, inasmuch as the real name was given in another part of the document. Nobble, still unconvinced, asked if Abelard was French for James. The boy was fain to confess that he did not know, whereupon his employer, acting instinctively on the principle, when in doubt leave out, suggested its deletion. The boy, still pleading for the note of fancy, offered to key up to it by another attempt to manage a love bird in flourishes, and his principal gave a cheerful assent.

The letter was accordingly amended in all these particulars, and, when transcribed with the same care as before, was thrown over the wall, the conspirators hiding in the boot-house to await an answer by the next garden post.

The nymph was not to be won quite so easily. The answer came immediately—indeed, by special lightning post, assisted in its flight by a stone— but it was all too brief. It contained but these words: " To Mr. Nobble. So you think I wear

a wig "; and it was without a signature. The con-
federates were in consternation : what could it mean ?

"It's that bladder of lard," said Nobble, in
scoffing allusion to his pseudonym; and for the
first time in his life, perhaps, he looked mis-
givingly at his guide. The latter stoutly repeated
his assurance that it was in accordance with the
best practice. The bewildered giant then, in des-
peration, suggested that it might be some cryptic
allusion to " the bird." The boy was still able to
defend himself : "Get out, sillykin; birds don't
wear wigs." "Wigs!" The word seemed to
flash illumination. "Read all that last part over
again!" said Nobble hoarsely; and he brought
his fist down on his knifeboard at the words "you
seem to have such nice eyes and hair." "Woa,
there!" he cried; "pull up! 'Seem to have!'
That's it; lay your life, seem—as though the upper
part o' the building might be only make-believe,
after all."

"Shut up!" said the boy, with the ferocity
of a poet fighting for a line; "it can't be that, else
why not 'glass eyes'; and she doesn't say a word
about them."

But the lover was sure of his reading. "That's
it, all the same. Never mind, old chap; pick up
the pieces and have another try."

The next effort was made in hot haste, this
time on pink note-paper, specially purchased for
the occasion at a neighbouring general shop. The

bird was now dropped by consent, as open to mis-understanding, and, for the same reason, it was arranged that Abelard should be changed to Jim. The letter, in short, was entirely revised so as to avoid all possible causes of misunderstanding. It was, however, written in too much haste to admit of much felicity of treatment. The author played simply for safety, and for his happier phrases he was indebted to a complete letter writer in his father's library, or to dim recollections of his own school exercises in commercial correspondence. The draft now came out in this form :—

"HONOURED MISS,—I am at a loss to dis-cover the cause of your displeasure, and am truly sorry to find that I have given offence. Nothing was further from my thoughts, I assure you, than false hair of any sort except compli-mentary in any shape or form. I have often admired yours : that was all I meant to say. I now beg to confirm my offer of a music hall any evening it may suit, or, I would say, any other kind of entertainment. I am fond of juggling myself, and, if you like that, would respectfully suggest ' The Wizard of the North.' Still trust-ing to win your confidence, and hoping for the pleasure of your esteemed commands. " JIM."

This time the answer was more favourable, and, to cut a long story short, it led to a conditional offer to walk out on approval, and finally to a formal. engagement.   Nobble was in ecstasies, and his happiness told on his work as well as on his life. His boots now shone like mirrors, his knives were simply streaks of sunlight, and his whole personality was transformed with the help of hair oil and of coloured ties. The boy had less cause for elation. His big friend had indeed doubled the fee to celebrate the happy result of his labours, but with this both work and wages came to an end. Nobble now conducted the negotiations by word of mouth, and the boy fell back into the ranks of the unemployed.

He was in this condition when his friend, one morning, brought him another note to read. It announced the end of the engagement, and called for a return of letters and presents without delay. The writer, it seems, had taken umbrage at a scornful toss of the head from a party—so she put it—cleaning the doorstep of the house in which Nobble served, and had jumped to the conclusion that she had found a rival, and that her secret had been betrayed. The poor fellow was thunderstruck : the boy rushed to the rescue at once. He wrote several letters, always at fees on the higher scale, to say nothing of refreshers in the shape of packets of sweets.

But the nymph was obdurate; there were no letters in reply; and there came a time when the knife-cleaner and his secretary had to rouse themselves for a final effort. The latter chose one of

his finest nibs; there were many drafts and amend-
ments; and they were discussed in the boot-house,
now transformed into a bureau. The knife-board
was dusted and covered with a newspaper to make
a desk, and, as the infant penman sat there with
his legs dangling from a washing stool, he could
feel the hot breath of his employer on the nape
of his neck. The boy, who was then reading
" Don Quixote," suggested, as one plausible mode
of address for the opening, the phrase " Fair
Cruelty," which he had found in that work. It
was, however, worse than Greek to the distracted
Nobble, who, in spite of his readiness to clutch
at straws, was able to dismiss it at once as " bosh."

At length the task was done. No legitimate
device was neglected to make it successful—the
issues were too serious for any risk of that sort.
It was written on superfine note-paper, bordered
with a stamped imitation of lace-work, and in
coloured ink. I regret the impossibility of giving
it in its complete form. The draft was unfortunately lost, and the Ratepayer was indebted to his
memory for even a fragment of its peroration.
This passage ran as follows in a cadenced prose,
which, as employer and employed read it together
a dozen times, seemed to be punctuated with slow
music rather than with the usual signs :—

"And now, Miss, to conclude, I have but this
to say : If, as I can but suspect ('expect' in

first draft) you are going to chuck me over (the boy struggled successfully for 'throw') for another young man, I can only hope and pray that you will not break his heart as you have mine."

It won the rubber; she melted, and, as a not inappropriate sequel to this process, she finally faded from the child's view with her happy adorer. New interests, new ties came into his life, and these two went out of it. He went home on one holiday to learn, as stated, that his old client had gone into the Life Guards Blue, whether with this bride or some other as his subsequent companion there is no record.

The Ratepayer is loth to believe that his old friend would have been a failure in war, though he likes to think that, but for his exertions, he might have been a failure in love, and that the lion of brawn was saved by the mouse of mind. The fourpenny bit he received for his last labours, by way of bonus on this completed transaction, was the last he ever earned in literature.

It is no uncommon experience. Genius in letters can rarely do for itself what it does so freely, so lavishly, for its kind. "I've raised thousands for others," said a begging letter-writer in a doss-house one day, "and all for a few six-pences and pints of beer!"

LITTLE RICH RELATIONS

EVERY family is a first family to some other; it is only a question of scale. The dustman with a regular " billet " is a capitalist to the odd jobber, out to-day after rabbit skins and old bottles, and in to-morrow with nothing to do.

Some time ago I came on the track of a woeful old wreck of an organ grinder, going out to work with his wife in her hobnails; and, following him up—according to my custom when anything interests me—I found that he was much revered in the Italian quarter as a successful adventurer who, years ago, had set out from his native wild to make his fortune in England.

Ah, that was the hard life! He was now a being as wonderful in his family annals as any of our own pirate traders of the past crossing the main from Plymouth Hoe. From time to time the people he had left behind got letters of his dictation, written by some Little Sister of the Poor, describing his greasy feasts in Hatton Garden, and representing him generally as the heroic figure of a dream of affluence. They wrote dutifully to him in return, enclosing photographs of the young ones coming on, in the hope that he might find openings for them on Saffron Hill. In a word, he was the rich relation of his clan.

The Ratepayer tells me that he remembers full well his leaving his boarding school—still in his tender years—to live for awhile in the country for the benefit of his health. The place chosen was a quaint old suburb boasting a fairly good day school. The air and the surroundings were matters of prime concern; so my friend was sent to board with a highly respected resident and his wife. They were childless; and their pretty cottage home was more than sufficient for their needs. They took to the boy, and they admitted him on moderate terms—for company.

It was rather a favour: they had retired on their means—they were careful to insist upon that —but they were old people and he was young, and that was the main inducement. Their style was rather inferior to that to which the Ratepayer had been accustomed, so were their manners and customs. Their aspirates were but effects of colour; they ate like the early Greeks. The boy, in his ignorance, was at first disposed to regard these things as signs of social inferiority, but he was soon undeceived. He found that his new friends were considered as persons of worship by the whole parish, not excepting the parson himself.

The old man had been a speculating builder on a small scale, and he had a substantial income from cottage property. His wife, in her day, had brought grist to the mill as a washerwoman to the gentry, and even, at times, to the nobility; and the horse and cart once used in her business was now called the horse and shay.

Their memories went back to the dawn of history; the old man had served in the Royal Navy during the second American war, and had been present in many a stout fight. The press-gang had pounced on him one night, on his way home from work, and had carried him aboard ship. His wife contributed to their stock of ante-diluvian recollections by her perfect memories of a time when the quality wore ruffles to their shirts. Quite a few generations of youth and age joining hands in this manner, might carry us back to the Norman Conquest in pure oral tradition, without a scrap of print.

They were not only the admired of a general circle, they were this in a high degree to members of their own family. They had been followed to their place of retirement by a sister of the old man, and by her needy husband, who earned a scanty subsistence by collecting the cottage rents. The position of these more fortunate dependents was one of vantage, inasmuch as they were always on the spot. The other members of the family could only come and go as occasion served, and when it did serve they still found their rivals in posses-sion of the chimney corner, as toadies in chief.

There were squabbles in consequence; and
sometimes the factions dispersed without shaking
hands. They persuaded themselves that this was
but the solicitude of affection; it was really, as they
themselves acknowledged in better moments, sheer
jealousy. All flattered the head of the clan with
lip service, and sometimes with offerings. His
birthday was a levee, much to his disgust; and
it rarely passed without high words. He bore
their homage with a grunt, which, however,
sometimes became articulate in a cry of " Cut it
short."

He was a good soul, and so was his partner.
They warmed to the boy as the only disinterested
person within range, in spite of the fact that he
usually had most of the birthday cake to himself.
He evidently cared nothing for their riches. He
cringed not, even when they asked him, on one
occasion, if he would like to know how it felt to
have five hundred pounds in his keeping, and
forthwith laid the lease of a small house of that
value on his lap.

He sat awestruck, indeed, as became his sense
of cosmic powers within his grasp, but the impression soon passed off and left no taint of subservience. He went back to his play as if nothing
had happened, and he received sixpence in return
for pocket-money, which it never occurred to him
to regard as a tribute to his independence of mind.
His own birthdays thereafter seldom passed with-

out his being allowed to nurse the lease as part of the treat.

Like many sailors of his time, if not of ours, the old man was superstitious. He regulated his whole life by a curious almanack, which gave predictions for every day of the year. It might be fair luck or it might be foul, but there it was set down. Such a day you were told was good for signing contracts, such another for making proposals of marriage. On a third you were to avoid lawyers, on a fourth you might set out on a journey, on a fifth apprentice your son. He looked at this calendar every day, as regularly as at the weather-glass : the two together were the intentions of the skies in both kinds.

But the almanack had still another attraction : it contained a full-page picture prognostic for the current year. This composition was highly coloured in every sense. The general idea of it was Britannia in full enjoyment of the peace of her virtues and of her rock, while her wretched neighbours suffered every calamity of storm and earthquake, blight, famine, and war. Most of them, in fact, were usually engaged in cutting each other's throats. All the bad luck was happening to them, and all the good to her. She sat there calm and unassailable, guarded by lions, whose looks threatened destruction to every foreigner.

It was not always easy to make out the detail

of misery on the plain below. The warring nations often lacked the definition of flags and uniforms; and the cities toppling over in seismic convulsion were at times hardly to be identified by their own ratepayers. But this was all reserved for elucidation in the .cartoon of the forthcoming issue, and there it was made abundantly clear that everything predicted had exactly come to pass. In this way one year's number made the running for the next, and the distracted purchaser of a stray copy soon became, in spite of himself, the constant reader. This was no light matter, for every number cost half-a-crown. The old man liked it all the better for that : his test for wisdom was that it should be a thing of price.

Less prosperous persons might find quite enough for their simple wants in Old Moore at a penny : with the luck for the year at his fingers' ends, he felt that he was up to every move on the board of fate. Many of the entries, no doubt, were rather beside the mark of his simple wants. He could hardly be supposed to take much interest in the warnings on the subject of proposals of marriage. Yet, such as they were, they threw a lurid light on the prospects of some of the unions of this sort announced in the newspapers; and his muttered " Cat-and-dog life !—cat-and-dog life ! " was a sort of running comment on the unlucky dates.

And he constantly found his account in the

entries of another sort. When the season came for his yearly trip to the seaside, he took care to time his departure for a date labelled "Begin Voyages," and he invariably had his reward in feeling all the better for the change. On days marked "Welcome New Acquaintance," he usually set forth on his periodical "fuddle," the only relic of the bad habits of his prime. In a general way he was a quiet, reserved man, with a taciturnity due more to asthma than to moroseness. His words were few, as became one accustomed to giving orders, and to taking them—I believe he had been a bos'n's mate.

But now and then there was something that stirred within him for the glow of the warmth and colour of life, for the sentiment of heart to heart and hand to hand, and its expression in canticles. On these occasions he ranged to remoter parts of the district, offering to stand treat to all and several, and sometimes bringing back a brother Bacchanal—sailor or soldier, by preference —to supper at his board. The distressed wife looked displeasure, but put off her observations on the subject till next day, when she knew she would have her victim at her mercy; and, after meekly supplying the pair with the means of revelry, left them to themselves.

Their songs presently shook the building with a noise that suggested choral rivalry between a saw and a jack-plane. One ditty enshrined a memory of the time of William the Fourth, the Sailor King, and, in the old tar's view, the last of the good fellows of the throne. His Majesty wants to put a stop to flogging in the Navy, and he goes aboard, after a frolic, disguised as a man before the mast. He is unruly, and is ordered to the triangles, but he refuses to take off his coat :—

> "I will not strip for to be whipt,
>   For you nor no other man, sir,"

They readily undertake to save him the trouble; but, as the coat comes off, they are confounded with a view of a breast covered over with the stars and ribbons of his daily wear. Tableau; and abolition of the practice immediately decreed.

It was a relic of a sense of the proper function of royalty, still held as a working hypothesis for the government of mankind by millions of our race. What is the kingship for, if not for championship of the oppressed and the righting of wrongs? The king is but the knight-errant crowned; and the king's good pleasure is to cut the knots of law and chance.

The uproar ceased at last, and the good wife had the beginning of her revenge when she conducted the jack-plane to the gate, and gave it a sly shove, which usually left it in the gutter.

In spite of all, she still looked up to " the master " according to the custom of that distant age. Whatever his shortcomings, he was a mighty bread-winner before the Lord. She remembered the struggles of their early time, and how he had fought his way up to the highest level of their caste. He was the employer now, where once he had been the employed; the master builder, instead of the man with the trowel. Good " tradesmen " at their craft often touched their caps to him. She forgot her share in it, direct and indirect, the more readily, perhaps, because she knew that it was not forgotten by him. Besides, he was such a scholar, though this really meant no more than that his ignorance of book-learning was still one degree short of her own. She applied to him for the spelling of hard words in her scanty correspondence, and he never failed her with his answer, whether right or wrong.

Over and above all this he had " made her a lady," by the outward and visible sign of a liberal supply of the stuff for the dresses which she never wore. That did not matter: there the bales lay, in the big clothes press, wrapped in their tissue paper, and ready to make up at a moment's notice in apparel fit for a queen. They were of all the colours, not so much of the rainbow as of the setting sun—bright crimson, yellow and blue, often without a trace of pattern to impair the force and the directness of their appeal. It did not affect the domestic budget: they were the savings of her pin money, for she walked contentedly in cotton all her life, because she knew that she could walk in silk whenever she pleased.

She was as proud of them as he was proud of his leases; and, in her softer moods, she would steal upstairs to show them to the boy. The master was never made a party to these private views—why invite needless criticism on a matter that men could hardly be expected to understand? Her infant companion admired without caring to judge; and that was enough.

If there was a third in the secret it was only "the smuggler" of whom they were bought. This person, who—as the boy afterwards had reason to know—was but a licensed hawker from Whitechapel, had acquired his wares quite honestly, and in the way of trade. But it pleased him for his own purposes to figure before his patroness as a sort of Will Watch, who had run the cargoes on dark nights, amid scenes of blood, and who was compelled to confess as much to her in confidence, by way of accounting for their marvellously low price.

To sustain this imposture he dressed in a sailor suit, and invariably appeared in a sou'-wester and overalls, even in the fairest weather. He carried his goods at his back in a mysterious pack, and his approach was entirely in keeping with his supposed character. It was usually heralded by a letter in these terms:—" Call on Wednesday, if agreeable,—Ben. P.S.—About 3," the last being

the hour at which the master was usually abroad
for his daily walk.

This, however, was less for her sake than for
the smuggler's, for whom the prospect of meeting
a brother sailor seemed to have no charms. The
day was as well chosen as the hour: it was that of
the boy's half-holiday from school, and it enabled
both conspirators to secure the services of a scout
who could signal danger or a clear coast at need.
The boy was duly on the look-out; and beckon-
ing the packman, as soon as the glazed hat
and pea-jacket hove in sight, he rushed indoors to whisper " The smuggler!" and to await
events.

The wary mariner abated no jot of precaution.
He rapped at the door with his knuckles, without
troubling the knocker, and when it was opened
stepped across the threshold without a word.
When they were all three safe in the parlour, he
invariably asked permission to turn the key in the
lock; and, lifting a corner of the blind, peeped
forth as though to make sure that no revenue
officer was in pursuit. The pack was then dis-
played in its shining glories, and the transaction
began with all its ins and outs of buyer's coyness
and of seller's guile.

" There y'are, mum! There was a bit o'
gunpowder burnt afore that was got in, but that's
neither 'ere nor there."

" A bit o' gunpowder." How it thrilled in the

boy's ears—until he knew, in short, until he became a ratepayer.

"An' please don't arst me 'ow I got it, mum " —he was, perhaps, most engaging as the culprit refusing to give evidence against himself. " No, don't arst me 'ow I got it. It's 'ere: that's enough."

" I don't want it."

" Don't say that, mum : it's the chance of a lifetime. An' don't arst me 'ow I kin afford to offer it you at one pun' five—'arf the price they'd want for 'arf the quality, in a shop. I got to get rid of it—there, will that do?—an' before this night."

" I don't care much about the stuff."

" I dussn't 'ardly venture to take it out with me into the street again. It's a 'ard livin' nowadays, with all them revenoo cutters worked by steam."

" Fifteen shillin's is all I could spare—even if I 'appened to 'ave a use for it."

" Don't say fifteen shillin's, mum : don't do that. Fancy you got a wife and famerly of your own. No, I don't mean that. I would say—in a manner o' speakin'—you understand. I'm that flurried you may do what you like with me to-day."

" There's the last you sold me still in the drawer."

" Lucky for you. Why, it's coined money as an investment."

"We've no call for investments 'ere," she said proudly.

"That's all right; but buy as many as you can, an' leave 'em to them as come arter you: they'll bless you in your grave; and may it be long distant."

"Fifteen shillin's is all I can spare."

"I couldn't go back with that money in my pocket to them as sent me. These goods 'as 'ad to be bought an' paid for over the water, even if there may still be something owin' on 'em on this side— don't you fancy anything contrary to that—and we must make a bit for ourselves."

A pause.

"I couldn't face my owners, lidy, I couldn't, indeed. What d'ye say to one two an' a half?"

She shook her head.

He began to fold up the pack.

"Seventeen an' six," she said, wistfully, as the bale was almost lost to sight.

"One pun's my last word," he said, as it disappeared. "I can allus drop it over a garding wall rather'n let it go for nothing. But it won't be your wall, mum, it won't be your'n, lay your life."

"Run upstairs and fetch my purse," she said to the boy.

Dear old woman, she too, like her lord, sang old songs to the ravished ear of the Ratepayer, but without needing any cup of inspiration stronger

K

than her tea. A song on the death of Wolfe was one of them; and in that Victorian era it was still consistent with her sense of topical freshness. She had learned it at her mother's knee; and her mother had seen the fireworks for Quebec. One more instance, if more were needed, of the ease with which a select few might reach the Conquest, joining hands. She sang it with full conviction— her voice cracked with feeling even more than with age. The Ratepayer can hear it now.

"Bold General Wolfe to his men did say:
'Come, come, my lads, and follow me,
Through smoke and fi-er—through smoke and fi-er,
Through smoke and fi-er,
All from our English guns.'"

The Ratepayer would fondle her after this performance, and call for "Butter and Cheese and All," as an *encore*.

This was an ancient jape in a kind of poetic horseplay that has ever marked our popular sense of fun. It told of an area-sneaking lover who had scrambled up the chimney to escape surprise by the master of the house. The master, who knows all about it, innocently orders the fire to be lit; and the trembling maid has to put the match to the pile. The melting delicacies from the larder, in the intruder's pockets, feed the flame; and presently he comes tumbling down to save his life with his "butter and cheese and all." Tableau! Just such songs, and of the same rude cast, are still sung at Christmas, on the Wolds, in our day, as they were sung in Shakespeare's.

> "And 'tailour' cries, and fals into a coffe;
> And then the whole quire hold their hips, and loffe."

So the old couple went down the hill together, as happily, perhaps, all things considered, as any two in history. They were sure of each other, and the rest did not count—the surer because of their flatterers. The poor relations plied the rich ones hard; and it was not all snobbery. Or if it was, then snobbery needs some new and wider definition—perhaps as reverence given on trust.

Where the trust is genuine, however misplaced, then snobbery has its title to respect. It was so in this case. The reverence was not without dignity, since—if only by way of exception—it was not offered solely for pelf. The advantage of having a rich relation is by no means confined to expectations under the will. He may kick you downstairs, but he is still something to brag of after the operation, and his harshness is an indirect tribute to your independence.

A rich relation uplifts a whole family, in an age of snobs, and enables the poorest and the most forlorn in his doss-house to pose as a prodigal son of affluence, and to appropriate the seat nearest the fire. The most humble of those in the clanship of the old master builder looked up to him, and felt the better for his being there.

Even his sister welcomed their occasional visits,

because they threw her own sense of opportunity into greater relief. Her hopes of getting the money in the long run were strengthened by the manifest conviction of her rivals that there might be nothing for them, more especially when one or the other stooped to court her for the favour of a kindly word. She accordingly reserved her most brilliant improvisations in this line for the days when she had them for an audience :—

" Talk of nightmares, I dreamt I see brother Thomas a-sleepin' under a tree, and two awful lookin' fellers a standin' over him with drawn cutlashes to cut his 'ead off. The wust of it was, I was stood rooted to the ground—there !—neither 'and nor foot to save his life; at last I fun' my voice, and I shrieks out : ' Don't kill my brother Thomas : if you must kill anybody, kill me.' And then I woke with my 'air on end—didn't I, Napper ? "—to her sleeping partner.

" That'll do, Sally," grunted brother Thomas; and the incident was closed.

For all that, he left the Nappers most of the little property in reversion; of course, only after the death of his wife. What else should he have done with it ? He knew Sally for a humbug; but her attention's gave the sense of power. She was his sister, after all; and what were the others but more distant relations, who, with her chances, would have abased themselves in just the same way ? It was all you had to expect.

His death was Roman in its composure. " Give my love to Sall, but don't let 'er come in," he said to the weeping wife. The message was delivered; and there was a commotion at the door; but it ceased when he added, " Tell her she'll be all right; an' push the bolt." Then the eyes turned, though the head was still : " Now, Betty, old gal, you an' me; only you an' me." The poor old creature broke down in sobs, as he took her hand. He held to it with all his ebbing strength, as though not he was leaving the world, but the world was leaving him to the supreme trial of solitude in the void. So the time passed for a space. " Bear up, Betty: half an hour more," were his last words; and, within the half hour, her hand was free.

IN LOVE AND WAR

THE Ratepayer had now to repeat the experience
of his friend Nobble, on his own account: there
came a moment when he, too, boy as he was, saw
and loved. It was a sharp attack. There lived in
the village a being—how to begin to describe her?
Oh, for a whole handbook of invocations. "Joy
to the Fair in highest Sphere": yet how tame
this, because it is other people's rhetoric; while
the only draught for this malady must be one's
own brew. The Ratepayer learnt as much, now
that he began to compose the letters appropriate to
the situation, on his own account. They were not
written on lines—he was out of lines now, and in
freehand; and mere echoes of the turns and tricks
of the old essayists were no longer to his taste.
He burned or tore them by the dozen: the floor
was strewn with his wrecks. He wondered how
the old ones, writ for hire, had served poor
Nobble's turn.

But this is still short of a beginning, and no
wonder: the baldest narration of it is so tremendous a venture into the superlative. " ' There was
a Ship,' quoth he ": well—how will this do?
" There was a Maid." She lived in the village—
I've said that already. Her father had an em-

ployment in town, and went to and fro daily. He painted escutcheons for the nobility, coats of arms on their coach-panels, and what not—herald-painting is the word. Her father's daughter did nothing—she merely lived, in the big house, the house that had two rooms more than the others in the cottage styles. Her parent was a stern, austere, remote man, and he carried his chin in the air.

Fathers with such jewels in their custody should be like that: it creates a longing for the prize: one visibly on the look out for eligibles would spoil the whole thing. There was no particular danger of this sort, in the present case. Had Sophia—I have named her—been ever so much on offer, the Ratepayer would have been out of the question: his age was but fourteen. Sophia was at least three years older; and, in regard to the Ratepayer, she carried her chin at the same angle as her papa's.

In her case, however, it was not disdain; it was merely indifference, so complete indeed that she once beckoned him as "little boy," asked him to carry a letter to the post, and offered him a penny for his pains. His first thought was to spurn the coin, his next, and the better one on which he acted, to pocket it without a word, carry it home with him, drill a hole through it, and wear it round his neck day and night.

But we have got no further. I have to describe

Sophia, to write the inventory of her, and here is not so much as a single item set down. How begin? There is the same difficulty with the rainbow, with Philomela in her thicket, with the lark on the wing. She was a part of creation, life—so are beetles, you will say—I hasten to add, a part of the glory of the world. Inexpressibly glorious, like light—I can no more. Her walk was a fairy tread. Forgive me, or rather, forgive the Ratepayer; I am merely quoting him. Her eyes danced with lambent fires, her small mouth had the curves of merriment; and, oh, the full, roundish oval of the face, and the little straight nose, recalling all the other rogues to good behaviour, a nose to prattle to by the hour, and to nip at times in sweet defiance of the law.

Yet this is hardly to the point, and it has been wrung from the Ratepayer only under cross-examination. Left to himself, all he cares to say is that the features were just " little beauties," parts of one all-pervading impression of divineness, no more. Items are not for things of this sort: the moment you begin to count your treasures they are gone.

What is a hero—brawn, might, majesty of devil-may-care? Nothing of the kind: he is heroism in the lump, and in the emanation, the one thing, the one word. Sophia was an Olympian taking a turn on earth—the missing link of the ascending scale between this and the beyond. She made the boy's school-books live. This, then, was what the old bores were gabbling about — bores no more — the anthropomorphic divine.

"But surely," I urged, "she was this, that, and t'other, in mind, character, powers." "How should I know or care?" cried the Ratepayer, "I never thought of asking such foolish questions even of myself. She was there; that was enough for me." He probably meant that we are all but suggestions for a dream picture of a highest or a lowest possible in man. He would have been the last, I feel sure, to deny that the wine she drank was made of grapes. For at this point, quite inconsistently, and still quite humanly, he roared out: "Oh, that mouth—to think that never once. Oh! oh! oh!" But I fancy this was but the afterthought of his maturity; and that, at the moment of experience, his raptures were without a taint of sense.

He adored then, and was happy, without a thought of privileges—the becoming frame of mind, or more than that, the only possible one for the attainment of the absolute in this kind. It all dated, as a pronounced and realised state, from the incident of the letter for the post. The Ratepayer had said no word on that occasion, but his cheek was crimson with ecstasy. He became one with all the great magnetisms of nature, with the sea in the freshness of morning, with the eve and the dawn. He was beyond utterance; he could only take the letter, look up at her for one delectable moment, look down in another, and make off. The upward look was the decisive experience. It caught a smile on her face; and the Ratepayer was another being from that time forth.

She had brothers somewhat younger than herself, both at the big school—not particularly alluring brothers, the Ratepayer had hitherto thought them: exquisite now, transformed, glorified as beings illumined by her ray. He made advances to them, and with gifts, for he wanted friends at court, creatures within her celestial orbit, who might touch the things she touched, and talk about her, or haply listen while another talked. But it was not to be: they had always regarded him as a person of inferior social standing, because he lived with the common sailor, while their father painted the coaches of the nobility. This time they made no scruple of telling him so: boys are such unblushing snobs.

High words passed, and in his wrath he challenged one of them—the bigger and a fair match. He was stung, that was one reason, and, for another, there was the singular feeling that he would like to hit some fellow creature, and to hit it hard, for Sophia's sake. I cannot account for it: it was, perhaps, some survival of the idea of championship and protection. Before she had given him the look and the smile—I say nothing of the penny—he had no desire of this kind. Now, with the coin as an amulet, he felt equal to the world in arms.

The challenge was accepted.

Then came a cold fit; the being he had defied was, after all, her brother; and what an offering for her angelic fellowship would be his bleeding nose! My friend was almost ready to apologise: I think he would have done so, but for a circumstance that nearly drove him mad. The pair had somehow guessed the secret of his heart—perhaps from something she had said; more probably from something he had said himself—and they played a fiendish prank on him. They made up a nosegay of weeds and withered flowers, with here and there a stalk of cabbage, or a frayed leaf of that plant, and laid it on her table with a tender inscription written in his name.

It was a truly symbolical gift in a way, for it marked their utter contempt for a fellow who could be capable of falling in love with anybody's sister, particularly with a sister of theirs. She was all right, of course, as a chum, as a being to hustle and play tricks on when the cat was out of the way; but to fall in love with: what an idea! He must be a perfect ninny, a born natural; and his state promised an easy victory in the encounter. His adversary told him all this, and signified that he was now panting for the fray.

Then a wonder: he flamed with fury, offered

to " take them both," and not one after the other, but at the same time. His eyes blazed with the shame of the thought of what might be, must be, her thought of him. All this did but minister to their sense of fun; and, in that supreme interest, they were base enough to accept the amended challenge, and to take him at his word. He was a weakling; and weaklings were made to be the sport of the strong.

There was a drawback, however : the head boy of the school, who stage-managed these things, had misgivings : it was unheard of—two at a time. One down and t'other come on, was all he could concede, though even that strained the unwritten law. The school sighed its disappointment—it would have been a memory for a lifetime—and urged that, after all, the challenge had come from the other side. The brothers promised to play him lightly, just for a lark; and, on this guarantee, the head boy gave way, for he, too, wanted a share in the memory.

The next half holiday saw the whole party in the lists, the Ratepayer, who had hardly slept in the interval, or taken food, facing the pair. His very privations, however, were the nourishment of his mood of combat; as they are with beasts in the wild. Over and above that he had a vision of the incomparable Sophia gazing at the disgusting bouquet, and feeling that he had used her ill; and this intensified into a deadly quiet his fury of revenge. He still felt equal to a world in arms; and he was the better for the delusion, for, truth to tell, he had no great technical proficiency for work of this sort.

As already stated, he was rather a sentimental sort of boy, with his more natural cravings all tending towards good fellowship with his kind. With one exception, which, perhaps, the reader may remember, he had hardly ever struck a blow.

His form was considered absolutely hopeless as he advanced to the onset, his arms hanging by his side, and with nothing but a nervous twitching at the shoulders to indicate any sort of readiness for action. The brothers, on the contrary, shaped well with both right and left. They came on, however, in rather loose order, partly because the younger was unfortunately taken with a fit of laughter which detained him, and made a momentary break in the line.

It was regrettable, for as soon as the other came within reach, the Ratepayer flew at him, like a wild cat on the bound, and dealt him a sudden, sharp, and altogether stupendous box on the ear that resounded all over the field. It was a blow with the open hand—such a novice in the art was the Ratepayer—and, if aimed at all, was simply directed at the entire personality of his antagonist, as though to wipe it off from the list of the troubles of life.

Yet this only added to the moral effect of it,

for the extent of the surface affected produced a report like a clap of thunder. I do not say it was heard in the next county, but it travelled far and wide. The dire and dreadful echo of it, as from neighbouring hills, terrified the recipient. He doubled, so to speak, on his own hinges, laid his hand on the affected part, rocked to and fro, while the Ratepayer, leaving him for the moment as one out of the combat, pushed on, to deal swift destruction on the younger in the rear.

That champion, however, immediately took to his heels, the Ratepayer following, the crowd veering round in a moment with cheers for the pursuer, jeers for the pursued. Then for the first time since the insult, the Ratepayer's mood underwent a sudden change. Offering quarter, he bade the other stop; and the astonished party at the ring side soon saw them returning arm-in-arm.

Their conversation on the way was of profound interest from a casuistical point of view. The fugitive at first sought to cover the reproach of his retreat by giving a sporting interest to the whole adventure. " I see your style," he said, as though addressing one of the masters in ring craft, " you swing your right, and land on the jaw." Now the Ratepayer had never known that he had a style, but this, of course, is only a note of the great art. He had imagined that he had but dealt a lucky blow, owing its force not so much to his direction as to the misdirection of another, who had thoughtlessly got in its way—such a blow as might have been given by the sail of a windmill in a moment of reverie.

However, he kept his own counsel, for it was too exquisitely flattering, and only murmured: " Yes; then I land." In his furious onslaught he had thought nothing of right or left, but only of getting at his man, but he would not have been mortal, at this juncture, to be able to own that it was only a fluke. " It is a good style," said the runaway, " and I've heard of it before, of course, but I've never seen it so well done. Let's see: you feint with your left "—the Ratepayer nodded—" and then you swing for the facer." " That's about it," said the Ratepayer; " it's my way of doing it, but I may be wrong."

The other mused awhile, and then gave the conversation a turn that took it at once into filial piety, and almost into the higher thought. " I shouldn't have minded much," he said; " punching don't hurt me; but there's father to think of." " Father?" queried the Ratepayer. " Yes; he'd get in such a rage if any of us got our jaw broken: bread and water for a week, and all that—see? I shouldn't like to go home with such a thing. Then there's mother, too: you know what women are?"

The Ratepayer trembled. " And your sister, too," he said; " I should never forgive myself if——" " Oh, she don't matter," said the other,

cheerily: "she's only a gal." "Only a gal"—
the Ratepayer's terrible right positively itched
for another swing, but he controlled himself.
"You won't tell her a word about it: promise
me," he said. "No fear," returned the brother;
"but she won't let on; she ain't that sort. If she
did, I'd——" "Mind what you are about," cried
the Ratepayer, with the old gleam in his eye.
"Let's shake hands," said his captive, turning
pale; "I'm sorry about them flowers: it was
only a lark."

The Ratepayer made no reply. He was in
an agony of apprehension: suppose the jaw was
broken after all, what would Sophia say? especially now that his vainglorious silence had
given grounds for the reproach that he had done
it of malice aforethought. He ran forward to the
group surrounding the wounded champion, and
found him still caressing the affected part, and
flushed with something that was more than shame.
What of the bone beneath?

"Sorry, old man," said the vanquished, holding out his hand. "Don't speak," cried the
Ratepayer, "just go on holding your jaw." The
other mistook this for mockery, and the flush took
a deeper tinge. "Would you like to see the
doctor?" said the Ratepayer. "Doctor be
blowed," was the reply, "it was only a smack;
and we'll have another go, if you like." "Not
for worlds," said the Ratepayer, with an im-

mense sigh of relief; "I've had enough." With that they shook hands on it all round.

"It was all an accident," said the Ratepayer, apologetically. "Oh, come, that'll do," said the head boy; "neatest thing I ever saw. Where the deuce did you pick it up?" "He's been tellin' me about it," said the younger brother; "it's his style—see: feint with your left, and swing with your right, and land."

The evidence was damning as to intention: in spite of the shower of congratulations, the Ratepayer went home sick at heart. If the flush persisted, Sophia would be sure to see it when she kissed her brother good-night. He imagined that sisters always did that, having none of his own, and there was a delicious interlude of rapture in the very thought of it. But it passed again, in a moment, into the mood of despair. And when she saw it, what would Sophia think? "Sponge in cold, old man, soon as you get indoors," he said, "and keep out of her way till dusk." The defeated champion gave a mighty guffaw.

They had kept their own counsel, or they had blabbed—the Ratepayer never knew—but whichever it was, it did him no harm. She smiled divine appeasement at their next meeting, as he hurried by, still with downcast head. That was enough: he might go on adoring, and it was all he wanted to do. To love for the sake of loving, and not to set much store on the return—has not that ever marked the furthest reach of this fine art of the skies? He wanted no more, had scarcely a sense of such a want, was as single-minded in it all as Fra Angelico, busy with his angels.

All the universe is implicit in a drop of water, all life in such a boy's passion for a woman beyond his reach. It was the womanhood that he loved in her, the all-womanhood, the something that was not himself, the sex in a word. And, since absolutes admit of no comparison, all the greatest settlements of the soul, in their fullest effulgence of glory, were in that suburban garden on the summer's night—Verona of the Capulets, Khorassan of the Tent-Maker, Granada of the Moors.

For a further note of identity, much of it passed under the light of the moon. There was a mound in the garden in which grew a small tree, and the branches of the tree commanded a view of a window that was hers. Here the Ratepayer, letting himself down from his own casement, passed long evenings under the vault, watching for the taper ray that betokened her presence. In this vigil again, he was one with the best: no heart could have throbbed with a richer intensity of expectation, no soul had a fuller sense of the bigness of all the issues of being, whether of death or life. Such, in favourable circumstances, is the start that nature has given to all of us: we begin as poets, though ratepaying may be our abortive goal.

Then at last, when the light appeared, what delicious tumult of the sense, what foolish fears of being seen and recognised amid impenetrable shades, as her window opened for a breath of air. And, if perchance her fingers wandered over the keys of her cottage piano, why, it was the soul of all the symphonies and all the love songs of the world. Most happy Ratepayer—and happy yet to be—for who can doubt that its message will return to him with all its immeasurable significance, in the final hour!

The tree was not only his hiding-place by night; it sometimes concealed him, and only less effectually, by day. It commanded the path by which she passed the cottage, and so gave him the chance of the fuller scrutiny of her features, for which he longed. The need of this came about in a curious manner. He had taken the drawing master into his confidence, though, of course, only in a general way; and, one day, when the subject of the lesson was "expression," had ventured to ask him for a case in point. The word really puzzled the boy: he understood line and colour as elements of beauty, but the other element was as yet a matter wholly beyond his ken.

The pedagogue was almost at as great a loss for definition, and he could only answer: " Why, the look, you know, the soul of a face, the what it seems to say." " As, for instance? " urged the Ratepayer. " Oh, you must wait till you see the great pictures, the great statuary; it's hardly a sort of thing that grows on every bush." "Has anyone in the village got expression?" ventured the Ratepayer. "Oh, how can I say off-hand?" "Have you ever seen Miss Sophia?" returned the boy, as carelessly as he could. "Sophia who?" "The sister of those two fellows at the bottom of your class." "Ah, yes, I know: beyond all question—strange I never thought of her."

The Ratepayer said no more for fear of betraying himself, but as soon as possible he hurried back to his tree, to study expression as it took its walks abroad. He watched for days, in the hope of rendering to himself some more critical account of the charm. " It's her smile," he said at last—still wondering what it might be, for better or for worse, to see her in tears.

" Does she ever cry?" he asked the younger brother, carelessly, when next they met. " Sometimes, when she's in a wax," returned the brute, only to bring the old look of fury into the questioner's eye; "but I can make her cry whenever I want without that." " You dare!" cried the Ratepayer. "Would you like to see it?" returned his friend, unabashed; "ask Walker: I did it one day when we had him to tea—the time I was ill with the cough. It was only for a lark: I bet a tanner, an' he bet a tanner— see?"

" Go on," snorted the Ratepayer.

" Well, when she come in to cut the toke, I pulls a long face, and pretends I didn't want to touch it, an' had a sort of feelin' I wasn't long for this world. ' What silly nonsense ! ' says she; but she drops the knife. ' It won't much matter to anyone,' says I, ' there's them, I dessay, as wouldn't lay a flower on my grave,' and looks her straight in the face, and clucks out a sort of a sob. ' You're a wicked, cruel boy,' she says, ' to talk of such a thing, an' I'll tell papa.' Then out they come, hot and strong, an' up goes her hankecher, an' I won the bet. I wouldn't have took it, but, you see, Walker wasn't my chum. Do it for you for nix any day you like."

" Stop," roared the other; " if you weren't the wretchedest little hound in all creation I'd break every bone in your skin." " What's up now, I wonder ? " mused Sophia's brother, as he hastened out of range.

The Ratepayer never spoke to her, never once in all his life. The case stands apart in the books, on that account. His gasp when he took the letter was hardly to be called an utterance. She left the village soon afterwards, to follow the flag as governess in some distant place—I think, Singapore—and the Ratepayer presently went his way too. Their paths diverged—that is the accepted phrase. She might almost as well have gone straight to Heaven, for the difficulty of keeping in touch with her. They had reached no stage of intimacy for correspondence.

How should they have done so? Think of the enormous disparity of age—he only a slip of fourteen, she full three years older, a whole eternity, if one allows for the difference of sex. She knew of his silent worship; he knew that she knew it; and that was enough for him. I am not sure that he would have asked even so much.

What a blessing for both of them that they lost touch in this way, each a planet in the very uttermost height of its ascendant, she for him a dream of flawless perfection; he, for her, " a nice boy " who served to teach her what some man's love was going to be, a lad of fire and force and passion, for all his innocence, and wearing a great heart on his sleeve.

It would have been a thousand pities if she had followed him in his tedious evolution into the perfect ratepayer, seen him learning to misdoubt the instincts of his boyhood, putting off the natural man of generous impulse, putting on—not without sharp wrenches of pain in the process—the other one of worldliness, caution, reserve, with parochial rewards. Whatever was to come they had lived one magnificent hour of glorious life, and were in a manner insured against the utter poverty of being for evermore.

LAW, PHYSIC AND DIVINITY

AT this point, for some strange reason, the Rate-payer left off talking about his childhood. It looked as though he felt that, with the Love and War, as I have called it, he had reached his highest in the heroic virtues. It was so, in fact, and he knew it: he had given me the story of his rise in the power of the spirit; he did not care to continue it into his decline. His shaping for life had been beautiful so far; and if he had kept it up, he might have got into the text-books as a good man. I could never learn more from him about his tender years, and my disappointment led to a certain estrangement, felt rather than expressed, on either side. I hardly wanted more, for I felt that the episode of Sophia was the beautiful flowering of him, and that the rest must all tend towards the sere and yellow. After that he had to cry, with the hero of Faust, " The earth has me again," or, more appropriately in his case, " It has caught me at last."

The question now before us was nothing less than the evolution of the angel, with which we all start, into the perfect ratepayer. No wonder he was reluctant to speak of the process of transition, though I believe he was entirely satisfied with the result. Perhaps he was hardly aware of it as a process, and life seemed suddenly to have plucked him out of his heroic age, and plumped him down into the Here and the Now. I knew that he had, in due course, done something in the City, I believe with success. I was also aware of a certain early-middle period in which he found it difficult to be off with the old love of generous ideals while still trying to be on with the new. He dreamt of great careers, the Church—the Army even as a second best.

Then came marriage; and with that he went over bodily into the art of getting on. He reared a family and started them in life on principles suited to their environment. He was now in City politics, and was considered to be on the high road to the Civic chair.

His great exploit in this line was the revival of the ancient Bellows Menders' Company, one of the glories of the past. He found it a mere name on a parchment : he made it an institution of great dignity, whose dinners rivalled those of the other guilds. Its beadle, specially selected by himself, was the tallest and portliest man within the Liberties : you could have run races round him by taking him in laps.

My old friend dined out every day of his life, in order to eat his way to the post of chief magistrate; and I understand there is no other course. The dinners keep the electorate in good humour :

an ascetic alderman would obviously ruin everything—an alderman addicted to vegetables and to milk or ginger ale, an alderman, in fact, of the Buddhist rule. The candidate for these high offices must feed on sterner stuff, if only to remind poorer fellow citizens that good cheer has not left the haunts of men. His guzzling is what the old divines used to call a figure; and every course is a symbol no less than a dish.

The Ratepayer I know took this view of it, for when we met again after our slight misunderstanding, I was struck by his outburst of wrath against his doctor for trying to cut him off his feed. That was his way of putting it. The doctor had ordered total abstention from the delicacies of the table for a time, and particularly from the dry champagne. When he was asked what about the dinners, and particularly about the toast of " The Bellows Menders' Company," he had suggested that, by a suitable arrangement with the head waiter, this might be secretly honoured in cold tea by the Chair. The Ratepayer had retorted hotly that he would be no party to swallowing a lie, and had forthwith called in another practitioner.

I said what I could for the offender, but to no effect, for I soon found that the aspirant and myself started from totally different standpoints. He was wedded to the idea that it was no business of a doctor to lay down hard-and-fast laws of health;

he was there to enable his patient to defy them with impunity. Any fool, so the Ratepayer was pleased to say, could tell you what to eat and avoid : it was for the physician, especially for the one in attendance on a public man, to show you how to dodge the consequences of indulgence.

"I'm not going to talk to you any more about my little silly childhood," my friend said, " but there's just this : I remember once at Christmas time, I positively refused to take the magnesia unless they promised that I might go on with the mince pie. I was not quite such a fool as I looked, even then."

It was a new view, amazing in itself, and still more so in its implications. For now it occurred to me that, just as my friend thought about the science of physic, so the vast majority of mankind think about all the sciences that aim at the conduct of life. In their view, for instance, law is a cobweb and the legal adviser is there to show the adventurous fly how to break its meshes when he happens to be caught.

In vain does the honest practitioner protest : he is still, in the vulgar view, the guide who knows the pass or, to adopt the favourite figure, the man with the ribbons who can steer the coach and six through the statute book. As a rule of conduct and a rule of right, law is only for the most insignificant of the little people, and a mere copy-book maxim for simple souls.

With such trammels no man of mettle could possibly hope to make his fortune in time to enjoy it. As it is, he goes into this good thing and into that, and he belongs to a dozen companies, with pickings in each—all dependent, however, on his not being hampered at every turn by the grand-motherly prescriptions of an Act of Parliament. It would paralyse the enterprise of the country. So " my solicitor " is expected to direct the plan of campaign against the public, and the other one in the silk and horsehair to beat off attacks, each receiving a handsome share of the plunder for his pains.

I defy anyone to say that this is not a fair statement of the client's position in regard to much of the legal business done in our day. The legal adviser may have the business or leave it, but those are the terms on which it is offered. I am trying to state the practical ethics of the question—say only as devil's advocate—on behalf of the perfect guinea pig who is also the perfect ratepayer. What can the poor pig know about the chances of that new mine in West Africa? It is on the Gold Coast, and if that is enough for his shareholders, it may also be enough for him.

The law in the abstract, the law in its quality of Old Father Antic, the party that does not count, may try to make him responsible; the man cunning in the law is expected to see him through. The adviser is engaged not as a guide to the Continuing

City, but just as the pilot for the shallows of the course in hand.

But what about the Continuing City? I mused one day, when the matter suddenly took a deeper interest in view of a serious malady of the Ratepayer that called us all to his bedside. The question naturally arose when the doctor began to shake his head, and I ventured to ask the sufferer if he was prepared. He was shy at first on this point, evasive; and I could get no more out of him than, " Oh, I daresay that'll be all right, too. I've done my little bit according to my means." I found this to refer to the fact, otherwise well known to me, that my friend was a patron of public charities, and incidentally a builder of churches, especially in new neighbourhoods that he was laying out in building lots.

It was clear that he thought this entitled him to full benefit of clergy, and that, in one word, he took precisely the same view of divinity as of physic. His parson was there, like his doctor, not to trouble him with tedious commonplaces on a misspent life, but simply to usher him into the Heavenly abodes and see that he got a comfortable place. He was the man with the passport, the friend at court, not the vicegerent of the dreadful Judge with the scales. My friend had made interest with the Church by a liberal support of her institutions, and he expected a return in kind.

The need for this soon appeared in the crisis

of the attack. The flesh had weakened, the mind with it; and the Ratepayer was in one of those moments of depression in which the pride of life seemed to have lost all its stiffening and to yield no support. What if there should be a something beyond that did not reckon as we reckoned, that judged by its own awful and immutable law, and that held the mighty as the mere dust of its balances? My poor friend bleated for a comforter: it would have melted a heart of stone.

There was no time to lose: we called in the first clergyman at hand, one to whom, unfortunately, the sufferer was an utter stranger. It happened to be, in every way, the wrong sort of man. He took his office seriously, and, bundling us all out of the room, began, as we afterwards learned, a most serious inquiry into the life of his " penitent."

The other yielded for a while, in his enfeebled state, and was led by question and answer into a most grievous recital of favourite sins that threatened to weight him for perdition. There seemed little hope since there was so little time, and the Ratepayer was almost at his lowest point when he was restored to life by nothing less than a miracle. This took the form of a sudden and healthy reaction of disgust against a consoler who could so far misunderstand the nature of his calling.

In fact, the vitality of the ratepaying nature was so strong in my friend that it enabled him to revert to his earlier idea of the priest as no more than a sort of Heavenly doctor, whose business it was to let bygones be bygones, and to " put him through." Rising with nervous energy on his pillow, he ordered the pedant of holiness out of the room, as he had ordered the other practitioner, and from that moment he began to mend.

I had the happiness of watching him through his convalescence by the seaside, and to hear him formulate a theory of law, physic and divinity— for, as it turned out, he was equally heretical in all three—which threw a flood of light on the new relation of these sciences to the way of the world as it wags. Like a true child of his time, he believed in nothing but the right to do as he liked in everything, with lawyer, doctor, and parson to stand by and save him from the worst.

We had many conversations on the subject, and each was to me a new revelation of things as they are. He was quite incurably of opinion that mankind are really governed by laws that never find their way into the copybooks. I had one day rashly extolled the life of reason, but he laughed it to scorn. " Don't talk to me of living reason- ably," he cried; " it is the one inexcusable folly of the reasonable man : try it, and see what will happen to you ! Did I ever tell you about that fellow I knew ? " And, without waiting for an answer, he began.

" It is a strange story, no doubt," said the Rate-payer, " this story of my poor friend Sam Filby, who, with all his wits about him, worked night and day to get himself shut up in a lunatic asylum, and had no end of trouble about it, too.

" Yet so it was; and for the simplest reason in the world. A chum of ours, as sane as you or I, had lately been snatched from the midst of us, and sent to a private institution of this sort. His name was Dunning. We had all three come to-gether at an army-coaching place, and the two of us left behind knew that Tom, as we usually called him, had not had fair play. In fact, we sus-pected very foul play on the part of his uncle, a retired major at the head of the coaching estab-lishment, who hoped ultimately to have the handling of his nephew's fortune.

" We had contrived to let Tom know that we meant to have him out. We felt that if we could come into actual touch with him and get full particulars, we could soon manage it. But there was no doing this in the ordinary way. Mere visits were quite out of the question: only long confidential talks could give us what we were after.

" Filby was naturally a plucky, forlorn-hope sort of chap; and one day, when we had discussed ways and means for the hundredth time, he burst out with 'I'll do it! What about shamming eccentricity till they run me into the same asylum? Then I'll get the whole story, and make England too hot to hold them.' "

" 'Absurd!' I said—you know people always do say that at the start.

" ' Nothing of the kind; the most practical proceeding in the world.'

" ' Suppose they *don't* put you into the same asylum?'

" ' There's no other within twenty miles: the same doctors—and they will be the same, no doubt —the same jug.'

" ' Ridiculous!'

" ' But do condescend to particulars. Why?'

" ' I never heard of such a thing.'

" ' Oh, as to that—well, I'm going to have a shy at it, anyway. I shall start shamming mad to-morrow; and mind you back me up.'

" ' I don't like the look of it; it's too wild.'

" ' Do drop thinking so much about yourself, my dear fellow. What about the other man?'

" ' But where do I come in?'

" ' In this way. Your line is that I've been " funny " for some time past, though you haven't cared to say much about it; and that I ought really to be kept this side up with care,'

"He quite knew what he wanted; I only half knew what I did not want: I needn't tell you the result. I agreed to stand in with him, and I was the only person in his secret.

"Next morning Sam entered into the business of losing his wits with the most stupendous gravity. He began gently to develop a fit of unreasonableness that would have tried the temper of a saint. He muddled his work, sulked when they tried to help him, and finally stormed under a wigging from the chief. He was clever enough, of course, to make it easy going at first. He let the storm pass off in a fit of the dumps that spoiled our whist party after dinner, and sent most of us miserable to bed. I wished him good-night when he was taking his candle, but he cut me dead.

"Next day he was better, only he wouldn't speak to a soul, except in answer to a question. He did his work, wrote his letters, but insisted on taking them to the post. And he broke up the card party again by spending the evening in what looked very much like making his will.

"They had the family doctor—not the mad one as yet—to luncheon next day. Our artful dodger veered round into perfect propriety for the occasion, and talked like a book. The doctor looked puzzled, the wicked uncle foolish; but as soon as old gallipots had gone away, leaving a confidential prescription for golf, Sam worked up an entirely

M

one-sided quarrel with the butler, and asked him
if he wanted to fight.

"'I wish I could see more into your game,'
I said when we met that night.

"'Why?'

"'Well, you are so off and on, hot and cold.
You're mad enough when there's nobody looking,
but the moment they send for a witness, you might
give points to a dove.'

"'That's my low cunning; the insane are the
greatest hypocrites alive. See?'

"The offer of a few days' rest put him in a
real temper, as threatening unnecessary delay. He
now had an upset with the major, about nothing
at all, and gave it to him with a straightness that
left nothing to be desired.

"Then they wrote to his relations.

"One of these came, a retired colonel, and a
good old fellow, but, I should say, rather soft.
With that Sam began his wretched by-play again.
He took the colonel by the arm, trotted him all
over the grounds, and sang the praises of the tutor
and his family. The old chap was mystified, and
it seemed a bit too deep for the others too. Still,
they never thought of putting Sam away, or even
of turning him out. I fancy they were unwilling to
have a second affair of the same sort so soon after
the first: it might have got the place a bad name.

"He wished them all anywhere for fools, at our
next meeting, and plunged into greater extrava-

gances than ever, by way of forcing the pace. He began to read all the advertisements in the papers —at any rate those relating to food and health— and professed to revere their authors as the witnesses of truth. There was nothing he was not ready to believe in this line, or to do. He spent much of his leisure in leaping over a fence as a test of the efficacy of his diet. And on the days when the result seemed satisfactory, he asked us as a particular favour to address him as 'Sunny Sam.'

" He changed his bill of fare every morning, and he may be said to have breakfasted on fads. When they offered him meat he pushed it from him, and wailed out a supplication for protein. He clamoured for nuts at the most unseasonable hours, literally threw a dish of asparagus to the dogs, wallowed in raspberry juice and mineral waters, and professed to regard his progress in the absorption of albumen as others regard their progress in piety. When he wanted another slice of toast it was always the idiotic formula, ' Pass the bread-stuffs.' There was no limit to it: he ordered a monster weighing-machine and a pocket tape, and used them at every meal. You would find him at lunch in his solitary chair, nibbling a banana, and waiting to leave off at the turn of the scale.

" When anything went wrong with him—and, of course, he took care that something went wrong

every day—he laid in quack medicines by the pail-
ful, till his room became a sort of museum. The
walls were repapered with testimonials, pinned
up under headings that seemed to include all the
ills in the heirship of flesh. Now and then he
invited strange beings to the house—understood to
be patentees—and offered them their own stuff as
light refreshments, not exactly to their satisfaction. He had tabulated five-and-twenty prescriptions, each warranted as the only way.

"It all went for nothing. The family were
startled, no doubt; but, if only for the reason
already mentioned, they made no sign of running
him in. When I met him, as usual, in his room,
he seemed quite out of sorts.

" ' Hang them ! ' he said. ' What more will
they have? I'm at the end of my tether.'

" ' Just what I think.'

" ' I'll have another go at 'em, for all that;
but I must change my tactics.'

" ' I fancy it's no use.'

" ' That's not like you.'

" ' What's the matter with it ? '

" ' To turn tail.'

" ' No; I only mean——'

" ' You only mean you've forgotten a poor chap,
your chum as well as mine, biting his nails off
in that horrible hole. I tell you it worries me in
my dreams. But don't forget this: if anything
happens to him, worse will happen to us.'

" ' My dear Sam, what are you driving at ? '

" ' He'll do something to himself if they keep him there much longer. ' And, if it comes to that —mark my words—he'll *walk*.'

" ' Banquo's ghost.'

" ' You tire me.'

" ' You are certainly mad enough in all reason.'

" ' Well, why don't you play up to me ? '

" ' It's odd,' I said, ' there was nothing the matter with poor Tom Dunning; and see where he is now! The bigger the crank, the better his chance of liberty, one might almost say.'

" ' Well, do say it—say it again,' he said, brightening up, as if struck with a sudden idea.

" ' What on earth do you mean ? '

" ' Never mind; say it again.'

" I did so.

" ' That'll do,' and he snapped his fingers and danced about the room.

" I felt really uneasy about him. ' You're quite sure you haven't been carrying this a little too far ? '

" ' Perhaps so; but I shan't have to carry it much further. Good-night ! '

" ' But do explain, won't you ? '

" ' Go away ! '

" His behaviour changed entirely in the course of the next few days. All the silliness and snap-pishness vanished. He was ' Hail fellow ! ' with everybody, courteous, gentle, hard-working to a fault. The advertisements were swept into limbo, the authors of testimonials were sent about their business, and the study of their works was re-placed by that of the 'Critique of Pure Reason.' He played his rubber with the rest of us, and altogether conducted himself with so much sweet-ness and light that a small dinner party was given to celebrate his recovery, and his relative was asked.

" It was a sultry evening, and the windows of the dining-room were thrown open. My friend and I strolled in from the lawn after the second bell, and he talked weather and non-committal items from the evening paper in a way that seemed to put the colonel entirely at his ease.

"As a mark of favour, Sam was asked to take down the hostess, and he smiled as though in grateful acknowledgment of the honour. Then, without a word of warning or the slightest change of countenance, he quietly threw off his dress coat, and offered his shirt-sleeved arm to the old lady, with a bow. She was too utterly upset to decline it; and, still discussing the beauty of the evening with the easiest manner in the world, he hauled her in.

" It nearly wrecked the dinner at the start. The terrified woman could hardly mutter the responses, and the colonel and the head of the house ex-changed looks of consternation. It was impossible to pass it over in silence, yet the major was evidently at a loss as to the right thing to say. At length he ventured on :

" ' Dinner first, Filby, billiards after, if you don't mind.'

" ' Thanks; but I don't think I'll play to-night, it's so warm.'

" In all my life I have never sat down to a more miserable meal. They didn't want to make a fuss about it, you know; but they seemed to hesitate between chucking him out, with his coat after him, or with the strait-waistcoat in exchange. He seemed to be thoroughly enjoying himself; and, as to conversation, I had rarely heard him in better form.

" The courses came on in a kind of gloomy procession, like that—what do you call it?— Egyptian banquet of the dead. He worked his way through them until it came to the roast, when he rose, with a bow to our hostess, and made for the door.

" ' Won't you finish your dinner? ' gasped the colonel.

" ' Thanks, I've had enough.'

" In another moment he appeared on the lawn, with his coat on, and staring up at the moon.

"'Aren't you playing it rather low down on us? ' I said when the wretched business was over and we had our usual meeting in his den. I was still ready to stand by him, but, I must say, I couldn't help feeling for the company too.

" 'I'm playing it according to the rules—the new ones. Ten to one they won't stand it a week longer; will that do?'

" I threw up my window before turning in. The wicked uncle was showing the colonel to the gate, and the dear old chap seemed quite cut up.

" 'Give him one more chance,' I heard him say. 'It would be such a dreadful blow to his poor mother.'

" 'One more, then, for her sake, colonel; but only one. I have my own family to think of.'

" There was a knock at my door: it was Sam, and he seemed quite upset.

" 'Read that—you see there's no time to lose,' and, thrusting a bit of dirty paper through the chink, he went back to his room.

" It bore just these words in Dunning's handwriting: 'Look alive!'

" Our hostess held her weekly tea-party next day. There was the usual gang—the baronet's wife, the lord of the manor's daughter, a drawing-room minstrel (you know the type), and a young fellow in orders, who was such a fixture there that we used to call him the curate-in-charge. The chatter was in full flow when, to our surprise, Filby dropped in.

" He said nothing, but he bustled about with the tea-cake and handed the chairs, and all that.

" 'You are very silent,' said the old lady in a rallying tone.

" ' I don't happen to have anything to say,' he returned sweetly.

" They exchanged looks and shook their heads. Presently he took up a volume of ' Half Hours with the Best Authors,' and asked us if we would care to listen to a rational word. And, without waiting for an answer, he began to read some awful rigmarole from an old *Spectator* on the frivolity of modern fashionable conversation.

" It was short and sharp work at last. The general practitioner called in the mad-doctor—the one who had done Tom's business—and even the poor old colonel was obliged to acquiesce, though not without a final effort. He removed Sam to a small farm belonging to the family in the same quarter of the country as our place.

" ' There's not much hope, I fear,' he said to me with tears in his eyes, ' but my bailiff will be there to look after him; and active employment may give the poor lad another chance.'

" It was no go. At the farm he went on more outrageously than ever. He began by raising the wages of the agricultural labourers all round, and, what was worse, giving most to those who were able to do least. A ditcher, with a family of five, who had rubbed on for years on fifteen shillings and his firewood, the current wages of the county, was instantly raised to a pound and his coals.

" At the same time an old couple, almost

bedridden, who lived mainly on a pittance from the parish, and scraps from the houses which they had to fetch in all weathers, were advanced to twenty-five shillings, and put under the care of a nurse provided by their employer. The milk allowance from the house was continued, but Sam actually carried it himself to save the old gaffer the toil of mounting the hill. This, by the way, made the ditcher extremely discontented. He began to shake his head over his master, with the rest, and to declare that he ought to be put away. In fact, he loudly expressed his readiness to 'go into the box' against him, should anything of that sort be required.

"The doctors and a family lawyer, who now had his finger in the pie, pressed Sam hard on this point. He was deaf to all argument, though always with the suavity which was the most exasperating thing about him:

" 'It will raise wages all over the county,' they urged, dealing first with the ditcher's case.

" 'So much the better; that's just what I want to do.'

" 'But it won't leave a penny of profit for the estate at the end of the year.'

" 'Then we'd better give up farming and take to something else.'

" 'The man was very well satisfied before.'

" 'He'd no right to be, poor creature. I assure you I cut it as low as I possibly could. Did you ever happen to look at the soles of his children's shoes?'

" ' Tut! tut!' said the solicitor; but one of the doctors gave him a warning look.

" ' The irreducible minimum, that's all I want for them; why, even now they get fresh meat only three times a week.'

" ' Stuff and nonsense!' cried the solicitor, losing his temper again. ' Where do you come in?'

" ' Only after the others, of course. But I've gone on getting board and lodging so far.'

" ' Very good, very good indeed,' said the mad-doctor, trying to pose him on the other case. ' The ditcher can do his day's work, after all; but what about the two old derelicts who can't do a stroke, and who get five shillings more—not to speak of jelly and port wine from the house?'

" ' You see, they want it more.'

" ' They're so entirely useless.'

" ' So entirely helpless, too, I do assure you.'

" ' Do you call that paying people according to their services?'

" ' No; only paying them according to their wants.'

" ' I give him up,' said the colonel when this came to his ears. It was as good as done now. Each of the doctors saw him separately, and wrote his certificate, and the certificates were laid before a Justice of the Peace. All three were for detention, and in due time he was ready to be taken away.

"It was great fun, I must say. They thought they were fooling him when they persuaded him to accompany them in a carriage for a short drive. He knew he was fooling them when he assented to their proposal to call on an old acquaintance, and when the carriage drew up at the door of the asylum in which our friend Tom was confined.

"Sam had expressed a wish for my company, and I was accommodated with a seat on the box. After the quiet completion of the formalities, in another room, he was handed over to the urbane proprietor of the establishment. They promised to call for him soon; he begged them not to hurry; and we drove away. I had no opportunity of speaking to him, but he gave me a wink of triumph which I shall never forget. And next morning I had a long screed from him which he had somehow contrived to get posted. Read that "—and the Ratepayer, after fumbling in a nest of drawers, handed me a letter yellow with age :—

"Glory! I've done it at last! I've seen our poor chum, and am hard at work on his case. We'll have him out in no time, and bring that old villain to the stool of repentance.

"But burn this as soon as you have read it, and don't give me away.

" It was slow work at first, I must say, and I was feeling as tired of it as you were; but, after all, the farce has given me infinite delight.

"And now for my secret—the secret I couldn't confide even to you for fear you should spoil the game. You remember that day when I was so down, and you said something, without knowing it, that put me on the right tack. What you said was this, ' The bigger the crank, the worse his chance of getting into an asylum,' or something of that sort. That was just it; I saw in a flash that I had all along been on the wrong line in playing up to them with mere extravagance and absurdities. My outrageous tempers, all my wild waste of good money with the advertised foods and advertised medicines, wouldn't do the trick, though they might have proved any man as mad as a March hare. They were willing to make all sorts of excuses for me, so long as I merely behaved like a fool.

" Then came your wonderful tip that gave me the secret at last. And the secret is just this: *If you want all the world to think you mad, you have only to live according to reason* —for that is what you meant. The moment I saw this the thing was done. We're all so frightfully sympathetic to eccentricity, so horribly hostile to sense and truth. As soon as I began to be reasonable they were ready to put me away. I removed a garment because I didn't want to wear superfluous clothing on a hot day: they shook their heads over me at once. I rose from table as soon as I had had enough, and left a dining-room with the atmosphere of a kitchen for the pure air outside—I was madder than ever.

"But where was the madman? Choose between these silly people stuffing themselves into indigestion and the wise man with a care for his health. Was I less wise when I said nothing when I happened to have nothing to say? Why, the finest Order in the world is founded on a rule of silence; and who was the sage who said that he had sometimes repented of talking, never of holding his tongue? My treatment of my workpeople capped the climax—in fact, it has sent me to the madhouse at last. Yet what is it but a touch of pure reason in human relations. You know the immortal maxim, the finest contribution of the ages to the science of being: 'From each according to his powers; to each according to his needs.' It is a whole gospel of the higher life, yet you have only to act upon it to find yourself in a madman's cell."

"We soon had Tom at liberty. Nothing could withstand the array of facts which his friend collected and smuggled out, and which I got published in the papers.

"That was easy going, but there was one drawback : it was quite the biter bit with Sam. They kept him in for a long time, and I thought we never should get him out at all. At first they said it was a perfectly hopeless case. It was all his fault, in a manner of speaking : you see, he'd pretended to be such a *very* reasonable sort of chap."

PIONEERS! O PIONEERS!

THE Ratepayer's story set me thinking on the martyrs of causes, and on what it might feel to be one of them. Sam was a martyr for his friend, and, as we see, he got very much the worst of it. The cause triumphed through his exertions, but he was "left." One may imagine the other acquiescing in his fate, though with a sigh, as he sat by the fire surrounded by wife and bairns. No doubt he kept a faded photograph of his deliverer over the mantelpiece, and made a point of saying upon occasion that he would not part with it for untold gold.

Now, if you come to think of it, all history is strewn with the wrecks of the martyrs of causes. No single cause as it stands in the completed record, pranked out with its heroes and its victories, but had its day of small things, when it was the craze of a few obscure enthusiasts hunted for their lives. The deserts knew them, and the scorn and enmity of mankind knew them, with the misgiving of those nearest and dearest, sharpest of all, and they found nameless graves. Then, when the proper number of them had met their doom, entirely without compensation for disturbance, the heroes came on to reap the harvest.

The pioneer work had been done, and all was ready for the man with the sense of opportunity. The pioneer band remained visionaries to the last, at least in so far as anybody thought of them at all, and few sought out their forgotten mounds. It would have been useless in any case, for they had departed, leaving no address in space.

So the passing moment seems propitious for an invocation to their shades, with the help of Whitman, whose eye they have not wholly escaped.

> " All the past we leave behind,
> We debouch upon a newer mightier world, varied
> world,
> Fresh and strong the world we seize, world of labour
> and the march,
> Pioneers! O pioneers!"

Yes; pioneers! O pioneers! how beautifully you died! Where you toiled in the wilderness there are now mighty cities, and the rich and the happy lead their not too edifying lives, without thought of a benefactor. The sequence of such experiences is the law of all the great causes.

First in the pitiless order comes the inspiration —the obsession, in a few minds, of the sense of new heavens in a new earth. Next we have their crusade for the achievement, with the contempt, the loathing, and the stripes that form their inevitable portion, and their disappearance into limbo as the enterprise begins to give promise of

N

a going concern. At this point we may look for
the advent of the business man with an eye for an
opening; and then, in successive stages, for the
triumph of the cause, the poets at work, and finally
the historians and the monumental masons, with
the dust of the pioneers still keeping its secret as
the processions pass along to the temple of fame
on commemoration day.

Really, it would be no bad thing to have an
All Pioneers' Day, correspondent to the All Saints'
Day of the Calendar, though in this case it would
be a day of the anonymous dead. For it is important to remember that the forgetfulness is as
fixed and invariable in the sequence as all the
rest. The true note of the pioneer is that nobody
knows so much as his name: the moment he gets
inscribed he loses something of the dignity and
pathos of his part.

Hence a certain mistake of the martyrs of the
Catacombs, in their practice of leaving cards on
posterity. They were too much addicted to handwriting on the wall. It was often, no doubt, but
a means of recreation, like the prisoner's habit of
carving in his cell. And, after all, it still consists
with the most perfect privacy, for the names are
useless now for any purpose of identification. The
inheritance of glory, power, riches for the cause
came when all these good people had passed, and
when the faith that they died for became a very
comfortable thing to live by for their successors,

Then, one day, in the fullness of time, we had
St. Peter's, and the gardens of the Vatican, and
the ordered majesty of the festivals, and the gorgeous Cardinalate, with its rare books, rare manuscripts, rare gems, and all else that belongs to the
life of attainment. The pioneers died to put these
eminent persons where they are.

I impute no blame to the latter for being there:
it is all a matter of the fullness of time. It was
not they who slew the pioneers, it was just the
course of human affairs. I impute no blame to
myself for being where I am—or where, at any
rate, I once was—"a happy English child," at the
expense of millions who perished under Roman,
Saxon, and Norman, to establish me in my share
of the national inheritance to-day. Only sometimes I wish there was a temple handy into which
I might drop in spare half hours to breathe a word
of thanks to the undistinguishable dead.

As we are all made out of the dust of the earth,
so we are all nourished out of the dust of one
another. Not the temple only and the glory of
the procession owe everything to those pulverised
forerunners, but the husbandry of such institutions
must acknowledge the same debt. Think of it in
all its details—the deeds of ownership, the deeds
of trust, the clothes presses for the vestments, the
tubs full of votive jewels in the cellars of the
Russian convents, the daily service of house-
keeping as well as the service of prayer, the

braveries of the Papal Guard, nay, of the very beadle at the great door.

It is all owing to the pioneers, and, as it stands in the completed transaction, it is the greatest miracle of the whole history. For it imports that you and I, if we can afford it, may be carried to that door in a cushioned coach, and may find everything in order for our pilgrim's progress from this world to the next, with the comforting assurance that the giants that used to bar the passage are safely manacled and under the eye of the police.

So this may teach us to look hopefully on much of the work now doing for the causes that are yet in the 'prentice stage. Great Russia is being transformed by the pioneers who are rotting in Peter and Paul, or in Schlüsselburg, or wasting in the Siberian mines. The issue is certain, for the order that has to pass away is unthinkable as a finality in human affairs. The great day is coming for that section of the race, as for all, though not to-morrow, or perhaps in a century.

And in that day when the millions have won their share of this brave world and its gauds, haply they may still be able to give a thought to the pioneers whose dust they shake from their feet as they dance in the sun. It cannot be a thought on the details of names and dates where none can possibly exist, for such seeming indifference is in the very nature of the case. It must be, at best, only a thought at large, a sigh for the poor fellows, men and women, who died under the sharper pangs of rack and thumbscrew, or who passed into Hades by the short cut of the lead mines to give the dancers above their heads their charter of greensward and tabor for ever and ever.

Our pioneers can hope for no more personality than the sands of the seashore. Yet one Russian exile, taking a pinch of that sand and reducing its items to a record, has made a mighty book of death and defeat, with victory still there in the promise of the skies.

Think of the democratic cause as it stands to-day in the parliaments of the world, our own in particular, its members men of worship, seated in Cabinets, and showing a shapely leg in Court suits. I have sat at meat with them in luncheon parties, overlooking the Terrace, where they entertained Governors of Provinces beyond seas and Secretaries of State at home—themselves in the running for the same honours. I say nothing against them on that account, for many—so rapidly do we move nowadays—were once of the pioneer band. They were of the pioneers who arrived—a rare distinction, but one that makes them quite ineligible for the honours of All Pioneers' Day. You cannot have it both ways, of course.

Then my mind goes back to the day of small

things, as I chance to find some faint traces of it in a copy of verses lately unearthed by a friend. It is a copy of doggerel in honour of some hero of the French Revolutionary time, and it is chiefly remarkable, if I may be forgiven the paradox, for the illuminating relief it gives to the absolute obscurity of the writer. He belonged to the second great movement of the '48, and he has passed clean away, no doubt into the privacy of a pauper's grave. He was a funny old character, I learned, and he kept himself alive by peddling shoe-laces and the like until it was time to join the majority of the nobodies.

Yet here was another pioneer, for our epoch was partly fashioned by such hands. He had striven for the six points of Chartist aspiration that now, won or yet to win, are but so many points of Collectivist commonplace. He assuredly had tramped to Kennington Common on the day of promise, only to find his way barred on the return journey by the guns and the troops in command of the bridges, and had finally straggled home to bed with a hungry belly and a broken crown. He, too, had gone to a dreary secular conventicle for his gospel, with its flaring gas-jet of the platform as the star of guidance for the unwashed crowd below.

In these and in their nothingness were infolded all the triumphs of the cause as we know it in our time—labour in the saddle, and no longer as a beggar on horseback; labour leaders the rulers of colonies abroad, and the constitutional advisers of kings at home. The finished product, as we see it now, with its courtly manners, and all the needful h's to its name, is but the flower of that earlier root now hidden in the mould. And, rightly regarded, the doggerel and the poverty and the grime of the pioneer band were all but an indispensable top-dressing of manure to bring that flower forth.

They suffered in those days for trying to send others to Parliament, and when, by the remotest chance, they happened to get there themselves, it was usually a martyrdom. I knew of one of these earlier working men, so elevated much against his will, and in spite of his gloomy forebodings of the penalty. He was a journeyman glass-blower, and he knew only by what others told him that he had a real gift as a speaker, and that his deep sympathy with his class was in the nature of a message.

One day they came to him to ask if he would not stand for the House. He scouted the notion, and, when he could think of no other objection, said that he had not the means. A whip round settled that difficulty, and he had to accept. But he would not be beholden for anything more than his bare expenses; and the week's wage had still to be earned by Saturday night. He canvassed after working hours.

On the night of the poll the anxious wife waited till long past twelve for a sight of him, till at last she heard his footstep and she ran to the door. " I'm in," he gasped, sat down, and burst into tears.   At five o'clock that morning he started for work, only to meet a disgusted employer and " the sack."   " Either you're a member o' Parliament or you're one o' my factory hands," said his proprietor; " you can't have it both ways."   It was the doctrine of the time.

When, in due course, our new member went to a Speaker's dinner, and saw the glittering table service, he could not forbear—" I helped to make all that, if you please, sir," pointing to the glass.

These little martyrs of the Little People still abound all over the country, at this year and day and hour of grace.   The moment you leave the capital, with its distractions and its all too abundant foolishness, you come upon them in quite astonishing numbers.   Every rural township has its serious men and women, potential sufferers for the idea, and certainly ready to work for it without thought of recompense.

The pitmen will think nothing of walking a dozen or fifteen miles out and home to welcome a lecturer who is one of the brethren of the propaganda, and to contend for the honour of putting him up when his night's work is done.   The best bed is his, or, where that cannot be, the best shakedown on the floor—the one near the chimney corner, and out of the draught. That is because they are all pioneers in their small way, intent only upon the cause.

This, I think, is the highest heroism, especially when it precludes not merely the reward of praise, but even the certainty of the prospect of attainment within the lifetime of the pioneer. Most of us, to tell the truth about it, need this hope of fruition for the day after to-morrow, and victory itself seems hardly worth having if we are not there to toss up our caps.

The first railway shareholders, subscribing with the expectation of quick returns, find beggary for their first dividend. Then their poor chances are bought at a valuation as bankrupt stock of hope, and the reward falls to a second holder, or sometimes only to a third or fourth. The first is nearly always baulked—that seems the law.

As for the first settlers—well, in spite of brilliant exceptions, their all too common lot is to fertilise their own fields with their bones. For when, with intolerable labour and anguish of disappointment, they have drained the swamp, fought inch by inch with stone and stump and weed for the mastery of the ground, and turned the cattle tracks into roads, they tend to faint by the way. Then all is ready for the conquering horde who are to " realise." Both have carried out the law of their being : the first had to fail that the second might flourish, and so it comes out right in the end for that bettering of the world which is nature's sole concern.

Why are some moths urged to death by their passion for light? Perhaps in order that others may not transgress the more benignant suffusion beyond the flame. 'Their dead are but the martyrs of the swarm—the pioneers, in a word—and their poet, if they had one, would have no concern in their fate. He would go on singing the light and its glories as an immediate passage to Paradise without a break. Whitman's little folk are to be happy here and now. " The world they seize "—is he sure they are going to seize it? What does he know or care? Then, as though the poem had been years in the making, and he had meanwhile learned to suspect a latent boss in the rear, he seems to pause to right himself, and to pat the dead on the back for compassion and for thanks :—

> " O, to die advancing on!
> Are there some of us to droop and die? has the
>   hour come?
> Then upon the march we fittest die, soon and sure
>   the gap is fill'd.
>   Pioneers! O pioneers!"

It is an admission, however gradual and reluctant, of the law working on the facts of aspiration and shaping them to its own ends. They have not drooped and died in vain. The remorseless world-bettering still goes on, though not for their profit, only for the benefit of—

"All the hapless silent lovers,
All the prisoners in the prisons, all the righteous
and the wicked,
All the joyous, all the sorrowing, all the living, all
the dying,
Pioneers! O pioneers!"

The more select pioneers have no illusion whatever on this point. Dust of humanity they are, and to dust they know they are to return, with never a taste of the happiness they are helping to win for their kind. These are the heroes if you like. All that is best in the present has been shaped by men and women of their stamp.

"What has posterity done for me?" asks the jesting ratepayer, and will not wait for an answer. Yet all the generations of the dead—that posterity of the hither side of the line—have toiled incessantly to make things easier for him; and his ancestors deserve ennoblement, as in a Chinese blazon, for every good thing in his grasp. This at least is a debt, and it is only to be repaid by service to the ages to come. You could sue for it in the very highest court, and many hold that it is ready to declare its full competence at the proper season.

But that hope is by no means the only condition of willing service for the race, for countless myriads have wrought without it for the something not themselves.   These are the pioneers of my theme, the dear Little People who feel that they are going to be nothing, and get nothing, to the end. Though bitter is that end for them, it may still be bitter-sweet if they know how to take it.   They have served the ends of God.

A LITTLE REST CURE

So nature has a use for all things, though sometimes she keeps her secret well. The case of
Martha Jukes, for instance, baffles me to this
day.

I heard of her from my friend the duchess—
I do not say this boastfully, though it may happen
to be to my advantage with the discriminating
reader. The duchess was no doubt a bit of a
faddist, but it was an amiable weakness. She had
derived so much benefit from a rest cure that she
determined to establish one for the poor, as a kind
of thank-offering. How nice to have them treated
with as much care as herself, and in a manner
wholly distinct from the perfunctory ministrations
of the infirmary, and even of the convalescent
home.

The Home of Rest was complete at last, sufficient to itself in all the perfection of soil, climate,
and sanitation. It stood on the top of a hill in
the country, commanding the most delightful views
of English landscape, all clearness within the immediate range of vision, all mystery and soft con-
fusion beyond—no bad image of the soul of the
English people. It was furnished with the sober
luxury proper to its uses, staffed with a visiting

doctor from town, a " local " to watch cases by day, highly certificated nurses, and with a cook who was the fine flower of the culture of domestic economy.

Nothing was wanting but a first patient, and at length Providence was kind. A denominational school, under the friendly patronage of the duchess, was being scrubbed one Saturday afternoon when something happened to the charwoman, a venerable drudge of seventy-three.

Nobody saw it happen, but she was found, by those whose curiosity was excited by the unwonted spectacle of an open door after hours, prone on the damp boards, beside her overturned pail. She had fallen on her battlefield; and, when brought to, she made profuse apologies for her mischance, and tried hard to resume the struggle there and then. Though this was impossible, Martha insisted on being conveyed to the back kitchen with the bed on the floor, which she called home, in the hope of winning her way back to convalescence with the help of the light and air drained off to her from the yard above. She promised herself to be all right again in a day or two, and ready to fare forth and earn the rent and things by the end of the week.

At this point, the duchess, on advice, stepped between her and the workhouse, and bore her off in a kind of triumph for the rest cure. It was no easy capture, for Martha, boasting that she was

" not done yet," struggled hard for another round with the Immensities. But when a radiancy appeared in the chamber later on, and, from the midst of it, a compassionate voice told her that all was ready, she gave way. The radiancy was the duchess in her entire personality of beauty, kindliness, and good nature. Martha had never been spoken to " so sweet " in all her life.

She had still raised feeble objections on the score of the back rent, and the breaking up of the 'ome, but the radiancy had disposed of both with a word and a smile. It had now to be a " yes " or a " no," as the duchess was starting for the Riviera next day, yet the old woman might still have held out, but for an overmastering willingness to oblige. Deep down in her heart was the feeling that, having received a kindness, she ought to do a kindness in return. She really did not want to go.

She reached the Home at nightfall, and, having been made comfortable, was at once put to bed. Everything was done for her, she was not allowed to lift hand or foot. It can hardly be said to have recalled her childhood, for she had a faint remembrance of having sometimes been cuffed into her clothes by a short-tempered mother, and out of them again. She woke by sheer force of habit at five, to start on her day's work, but the deep " hush ! " of the nurse reminded her of the true state of affairs, and she at once went off to sleep again.   It seemed like sinking into bottomless depths of rest.

At ten her eyes opened in shame on the streaming light of the hour.   She was for jumping up at once, but the nurse told her she must lie still, and have herself washed and put to rights for breakfast in bed.   She had not breakfasted in bed for over thirty years, on the birth of her last, and she wondered what it would be like.

It *was* nice—so " softish like," as though the fight was over, and you were looking down on things from the sky, easy in your mind.   Waited on hand and foot!   What a strange sort of feeling!   And the nurse was so pleasant in her way of speaking, and called her " my dear "—another thing she did not get much of nowadays.   It was mostly " Jukes " with the people that gave her the odd jobs; and, at the very best, " old gal."

The doctor was just as nice as the nurse, a real gentleman; you could tell it by his necktie, and by his way of sounding his words, and so on— " every inch of him," that was what she meant to say.   He said, " Well, how are we getting on ? " first go off, and kept it up like that all through. She wondered if he knew what a poor old " nobody-cares-for-me " she was, or whether he thought she was a lady.

What a strange new world, to be sure!   And to think there might be people who talked to one another like that all day long, and perhaps all the year round, and never swore or told you to " come out of it ! " What a strain upon them, to be sure ! The doctor said she must keep still, and have everything done for her. And when she put the question to him that she could not help putting, though she might have known, he said it was all paid for, board and lodging, and even the nice bright fire in the grate and the big scuttle of coals—" bests," anybody could see that by the way they burned.

There was one thing that rather disappointed her—the doctor didn't send any medicine. All he said was that she was to eat just as much as ever she could, and get her strength up. And when she asked him what about the exercise, he said they would give her " message "—that was the word, as well as she could make out—and it would do quite as well.

Message ! What could that be ? Well, presently the nurse came in and threw off the bed-clothes, and told her to keep still, and then began pulling her about in the strangest way she'd ever heard of in all her life. It was a sort of gentle punching all over her body; no, not so much that as a sort of kneading, as though you were making puddings, and with that a rubbing till you felt as tired as if you'd done a hard day's work. Well, that sent her off to sleep again till something jingled and tinkled that woke her up, and it was

o

nurse coming in with a tray all covered with things to eat.

" Dinner already; oh, I couldn't touch a mor——"

" No, not dinner; only luncheon; dinner by-and-by." Then nurse propped her up with pillows, and brushed her hair again, and washed her hands. Oh, that scented soap!—like the smell of a better world.

Then nurse put the tray on a curious sort of table that went right across the bed, and said, " Eat away."

" I couldn't, deary, I really couldn't so soon. All I'm used to is a bit of bread and cheese in the middle of the day."

" That won't do here," said the other. " Don't you see the eating is to make you strong, and the massage is to give you exercise, so that you can eat more. It's the treatment."

With that she lifted the cover off the dish, and there was a small pile of cutlets—" baby chops, I call 'em," mused the old woman; " pictures, too, with their clean cuffs at the ends made out of frilled paper to hide the bone." A cuff like that had come to her share once when they distributed the broken victuals after Lord Mayor's Day. She had kept it for a time, as a curiosity. She wanted to tell the whole story, but nurse said she mustn't talk much, or do anything else, except eat and drink—" doctor's orders."

She kept quiet for a time, but still her eyes were wide open; and at last nurse asked if there was anything the matter. So she plucked up spirit for it, and said she was lonely in her mind.

Nurse asked her if she ever read a novel.

" What was that ? "

" Well, a story."

She said her eyesight was bad, but presently she thought she had better tell the truth about it, before they found her out. So she owned that she did not know how to read.

" Why not let me read for you ? " the other said. " What sort of story would you like ? "

Martha didn't want no stories : there was plenty of them going round every day in the place she came from—" jest you live in a court ! And besides, the stories in the court was true : it wouldn't be much fun crying over a lot of lies."

So nurse took up her knitting and began to hum a little tune. Somehow that must have sent Martha off again, though she hardly knew how or why. All she remembered was a feeling as if she was dying, though dying easy, when people went off, with all their relations gone, and nothing on their mind. She had seen it scores o' times when she had been nursin', herself, and had laid 'em out afterwards, still with the smile on their faces.

By-and-bye there was the jingle and the tinkle again, and this time it was tea. First she said she had no appetite, and then she began to peck a bit. It looked so nice—toast on a little plate, with a cover on, and all the crust cut off; and a pat with parsley round it, if you wanted any more butter; and " paste in a pot with a little picture on the lid that tasted like s'rimps."

Well, well, what a trouble gentlefolk must give to servants : no wonder they wanted so many of 'em. The tea was delicious; she had never drunk anything like it; and two jugs, one with milk in it, and the other !—well, you could stand a spoon up-right in it—real cream ! Three penn'orth, if it cost a farthing, and nurse tilted half of it into the cup before Martha could say " Jack Robinson." Oh ! It made the tea, like everything else here, kind o' velvet—like the bed and the carpet and the way the people treated you, and the way they talked, and the quiet of the whole place.

It was as if all the hard luck had gone out of life. The very air that came in from the garden seemed to whisper in your ear like mother's prattle to a new-born babe. " You know," said Martha, explaining to the nurse, " the silly talk afore it's time to turn out to work again, and the little un's all her own for the pettin'." Even when the window was shut, there were still flowers on the table—" big bokays of 'em, as sweet as the soap." What a world !—just like the place they talk about at the Mission Hall.

More sleep, more " message " after that, and now nurse asked her what she could fancy for her supper—dinner she called it, but it was all one. Then Martha was obliged to show that, bound 'and an' foot like, as she was, she had her rights. She was a bit cross, and she said, " nothing if she died for it "; and nurse gave way, still with her beautiful smile.

" No hurry," she said; " you'll do better to-morrow; this is only the first day."

Well, to-morrow it was worse than ever—for luncheon a pullet stuffed with cooked rice, and, as Martha described them to herself, " little black things in it that tasted like the smell of fresh earth, and served on thick toast, with more of the little black things, kind of dancin' attendance on it, all round the dish." And after that she had to rest for half an hour with her eyes closed. To rest before you were tired!—it was about her first stroke of hard work since she entered the place.

" Don't lay so stiff," said the nurse; " make your limbs lissom, and try to feel you are not doing anything anywhere in all your body or soul. Fancy it's a Bank Holiday."

" I always scrub out offices that day—morn-ings," said the patient; " gentleman of the name of Filter. He——"

" Well, never mind him," said nurse; " let your-self go all over, like as if you were in a sea of warm water. What are you pulling at the bed-clothes for? "

The poor creature was really trying to feel that

she was in the sea, and it ended naturally in her having to clutch at something to save herself from going down.

" Do you know what I've been thinking of, nurse ? "

" No; and please don't tell me. Your thoughts must be in warm water too."

Soon her attendant began to dress her, and then, for the first time in her life, Martha learned the uses of a lady's maid. All her garments were taken up one by one from their snug place before the fire, and put on with absolutely no effort of her own. Her hair was brushed for her—just like dressing a baby, she said to herself—and beautiful new slippers were fitted to her feet, while the limbs were carefully lifted for the purpose to save her the fatigue of muscular exertion. Then she was led to her arm-chair, and gently lowered into it as though she were a kind of " glass with care." Tea-time brought the trial to a close; after that she was undressed again with exactly the same precautions against the expenditure of energy, and put to bed.

Martha now began to have deep searchings of heart about the wickedness of her new way of life. Eating as much as you could, and working as little as you could—it was a reversal of all the values of her simple experience; and for her at least the old way was immutable as doom. It might be right for the others : they had money, and could do as they liked.

In her code even leisure—she knew nothing of idleness—was a crime that automatically entailed its own punishment. Lose an hour and you lost tuppence; and then what about the bite and sup at the end of the day? Her Providence was but a task-master wielding a seven-tailed cat for those who shirked their work. Now, it was all very well to say that for the passing moment everything was paid for: that could not possibly last, and, besides, the right and the wrong of it still remained. People like her—and most people she thought were of her sort—they *were* " people "; the others were only gentlefolks—were not made for such a life. They were made to stick at it as hard as they could for ever, just as horses were made for pulling cabs and such-like—see how exactly their bodies fitted the shafts—and it was no use going against the way things was meant to be.

So she had never been quite idle, even when her work for a living was done. When she came home at night to her tea and bread-and-butter, before turning into bed, she still fumbled at some sort of labour, mainly for the sake of keeping her hand in. As for eating as much as you could, that was positively foolish: the right way was always to leave off before you had quite done, so as to have something in the cupboard, if the worst came to the worst. Anything would do, even a bit of dry bread : it was a kind of charm.

It was this very thought of the something left

over that made her so uneasy now. She could
not possibly eat all that was brought to her, but
what became of it when it was sent away? Wasted,
no doubt; thrown to the pigs: she had heard of
such doings at establishments mounted on this
scale. Now if only she might be allowed to keep
it, and dole it out to her friends! Why, that tart
sent down yesterday, with only a single gap in it,
would have made a wedding feast in her court.
As for the children, oh!—and the tears came into
her eyes—half a dozen of 'em could have been kept
going, especially with breakfast before they went
to school, with what was sent away from her board.
She spoke to nurse about it next morning, and
offered to give names and addresses.

But nurse simply said it was against the rules;
and, at the same time, urged her to leave off worrying about anything at all, or she'd never get well.
To leave off worrying! How could she possibly
do that? Why, worry, hurry, and fear was her
principle of being. It roused her in the dark
winter mornings; the tic-tic of it in her dreams
was her alarum clock; it keyed her up to all the
work of the day, and made her keep a civil tongue
in her head under every rebuff.

If only they would let her get up and do some
of the work! Perhaps nurse, as well as doctor,
didn't know what an old thing-of-all-work she really
was. The lady who sent her in and paid for her
might have forgotten to tell them, and they might

fancy she was a bit of a lady herself—brought up
to do nothing, and taking to it kind. Then what
would nurse say when she found out? Might it
not be better to make a clean breast of it once for
all?

"You must not think I'm used to bein' waited
on," she said; "I've 'ad to work for my own
livin' ever since I was——"

It was no go: the other would not take the confession. "Will you keep still, please, still all
over?—this place is for the rest cure."

With that, as a sort of last chance, she fell back
on the plea of her self-respect. "I think I ought
to do somethin' towards my keep; p'raps you
wouldn't mind my washin' up after meal times."

"Be still, still, still," said nurse, laying a finger
on the bloodless lips.

It must be done by stratagem, then; so she lay
perfectly quiet, and closed her eyes until her gaoler
left the room. Then she jumped up, and began to
dress, vaguely as to any purpose beyond that, but
still with a hope of finding something to do. The
other returned unexpectedly in the midst of it, and
this time was moved to strong displeasure. "How
dare you put on your stockings by yourself! I
won't be answerable for it—there!" Her tone
seemed to portend immediate resignation—perhaps
a letter to the duchess, who frequently wrote for
news. Martha dropped the offending garment,
begged pardon, and went back to bed.

But the outburst passed as quickly as it came, and nurse was just as good as gold again. She sat by the bedside, and talked to the wondering listener by request about the lives of other people who had gone through the cure under her care. They earned their title to repose by their tremendous exertions in the world of fashion. Balls, parties, races, visits, and what not, made them " rags " at the close of the season, and but for establishments of this sort, the whole population of the Red Book might perish before its time.

Twenty-four hours of the vortex—it was an awful round; and it left you like a skeleton, if you didn't take care. It was bad enough for the maids, but what must it be for the mistresses ? The others, the selfish things, often grumbled and looked sleepy on purpose when they were kept up a bit late. But, if they were not there, who would undress their charges, and warm the " night-cap " of milk or beef-tea which was indispensable to their repose ?

Women of fashion had to throw themselves into a chair and let everything be done for them—just like prize-fighters between the rounds, so nurse had heard say—everything, garment by garment, taken off as tenderly as layers of dressing from a wound. In their overwrought state anything might happen.

In spite of all precautions, one of her patients had caught cold on leaving a heated ball-room, and it fastened on her so that she had to be sent all round the world for her rest cure, with nurse in charge. Yes, all round the world. The husband was a great yachtsman, and he had the poor thing carried to the train, and carried aboard, and there she lay, with just a little getting up now and then, while all the glory of foreign parts passed in panorama before the windows of her state-room. It was a very narrow escape indeed, for the cold clung to her all through the Mediterranean, and only parted company at the other end of the Suez Canal. It·was a sort of tickling in the throat— some thought owing to too many cigarettes.

" They should have tried a gargle," said Martha simply; but nurse waved the suggestion aside.

" Bless you, she was far beyond that: there were times when we thought we should hardly bring her round. But she had a wonderful constitution, and we were able to take her ashore sometimes, and carry her through some of the pretty places in a sort of litter, with natives walking at a footpace. The massage and the feeding did it, just as it is going to do it for you, if you keep quiet and do what you are told."

Nurse did enjoy that voyage, especially the dawns and the sunsets at sea—nothing equal to them on land. And then all the extraordinary people—some with turbans, but, beyond that, almost as naked as they were born, and spending most of their time in saying their prayers.

Her revolt suppressed, Martha settled down to make the best of it, not without an occasional longing for things dear to her in the old life. There was the little mug on her chimney-piece, inscribed in gold letters "A Present from Margate," and adorned with a view of the port. She wished she could have it here. It was prettier than all the pictures in this room put together. Her husband had won it for her in a cock-shy years and years ago, when they were afield for the hop-picking, and she always had her tea out of it on her wedding day. This recollection served to throw her into a reverie on her past life, which was as near as she could get to thinking on nothing, according to the rules.

There was so little to think about but a monotony of grinding toil, though she was hardly aware of that. She was born into drudgery; her very playtime in the gutter had been but a criminal interlude of the serfdom of child labour, duly punished with slaps. She "went arrands" almost as soon as she learned to walk; and the chief events of her infant experience were but changes in the proprietary of chandlers' shops. One firm gave a bonus of an acid drop to every purchaser of goods to the value of twopence, another did better business with the offer of a toy.

Soon it was time to go out to that hardest of all service, in which your very masters are themselves of the slave class, and you are servant of servants among the poor. She became general drudge in a lodging-house, where she was kept at it from morning to night, at wages that hardly paid for her shoe-leather. The next great change, that marked the adult stage, was the setting up " on her own " as a charwoman of offices. It was different from other work of its kind in its solitude and general self-effacement. You had to scrub the floors, dust the desks, and make all tidy for the gentlemen, but to take care never to be seen by any of them; and it had the strange effect of confining your main interest in existence to what was under your feet.

In the more " upright " callings—well, you still had a peep at the sky now and then, if only of as much of it as roofed the space between the walls of the court. But now it was deal boards for ever —nothing but that, miles and miles and miles of 'em, if put all together length and breadth. It was as though you might say you had scrubbed all London in your time. She wondered if any-body had ever seen more of London in that way than she had. It was wonderful what differences there were in the knots of deal wood when you came to study them with care.

Then, in due and inevitable course, came " housemaid's knee." This, however, as it turned out, was a sort of holiday, a break in the monotony, for it took her to the hospital, and gave her a glimpse of the heroism of suffering in her class. She was among the out-patients, in the great rush of the dinner-hour, when scores of women came in to have the most horrid cuts and burns and bruises attended to, and to get back to work without losing time. And so, still scrubbing on, she added all Birmingham, in superficial area, or all Manchester, to her previous conquest of all London.

Marriage was her next milestone of memory. The chief inducement to it was that it promised a bit of a change. He was hawking flowers at the area railings, and, after furtive glances, he at length ventured to pass the time of day. A fortnight after they were off to the hop-fields for the honeymoon. That was new life: the open country, the fresh air, the sing-song on Saturday nights in the rural beershops; and, as they walked home, the great vault above and its stars, with no end to it on either side.

Then back to the big city for long, long years to keep house for her man, and bear and bring up the children. He was not a bad man, but he was chronically out of work, and that sometimes made him savage. He had no trade to his fingers, that was how it was, and nobody wanted him very much. When things were in this state she returned to the boards again, and scrubbed—say all Liverpool—to add to the honours of her record. It was not so easy now, with nobody to look after the children, but they pulled through—all except one, the second of the three boys, who got into bad company and died in jail.

One of the others went for a sojer, and was killed in battle. She hoped it was only an accident, but there—he always was that " not to be daunted like "; and it was not for her to think the wuss of him, even if he'd brought it on himself. She couldn't say where the battlefield was, to save her life, but she was sure it was her boy, because they'd sent her home the things they found in his pockets, and she knew the locket on his chain.

Meanwhile the father was run over one night when he was a bit the worse, and the daughter married and went out to Australia, hundreds and hundreds of miles away. She wrote regular till the letters stopped all of a sudden, and what became of her or her husband the old mother never knew. Perhaps something happened to her, and the husband lost the address. A district visitor wrote to the postmaster, but the answer was " Gone up country eighteen months ago," and that was all.

The other son got a steady job, and kept it for years—something in a chemist's, not a shop where they sold physic, but a sort of factory where they made it. He washed out the bottles and swept the floors and such-like. So he and she kept house together, and a good boy he was to her until he lost his place through a saucy word to his master. Pore feller! " sperrit " was his fault, too, though the only one, but perhaps if he'd done wuss in failin's he might have done better in life. It's no use speakin' up unless you've got money behind you; that was what she'd learnt, and about the only thing. He was no good for any other trade, and he was out for months.

With that she had to work harder than ever, though her knee had " come on again." Still, it might have been worse, for there was at least the work to do—a mission-hall Saturdays, and a club-room of the Social Democratic Federation first thing Sunday morning. It broke his 'art like to have her keeping him, and he never would be beholden to her for anything more than his break-fast and his bed—both in the one room, which was all they could afford now. How he managed for the rest she never knew, but sometimes he came home like a 'ungry wolf, and then she made him share her herring, and they both had a good cry. One day he drowned himself in the 'Am-stead Ponds, and there was an inquest, and nothing in his pockets but a few lines to her on the edge of a newspaper. He was buried by the parish, without a stone to show where he was laid; but, whenever Bank Holiday came round, she spent the afternoon at the pond.

So it went on till she broke down that day at her work, and the lady found her, and she was brought on here for the rest cure. That was her life. She had hardly given a thought to it till now. Not but what it might sometimes have come into her head, though she had been too busy to work it out.

So the days passed, and Martha began to think that the rest cure might not be such a bad thing after all. This was the beginning of a great change, at first to resignation, and finally to full acceptance and delight. She gradually ceased to struggle, and she willingly became a passive instrument in the hands of doctor and nurse. They fed her for strength, they gave her " message " for exercise, they kept her mind a blank for peace and quietness, and she lost the habit of anxiety and the count of time.

It came, not all in a moment, but bit by bit, till at last she learned to regard this as *the* life, and the other as the dream—this, to be waited on, coddled, humoured, and never to have to move hand nor foot. " Where the weary are at rest "—what a lot that might mean ! not the mere stillness of death, but rest, knowing you were resting. All the old resolutions of combat simply vanished before that soothing thought. They were " onnatural ": people were not meant to be always at it, morning, noon, and night, with the grave for their first day off.

Self-assertion was the next stage; she grew exacting, imperious even, in her demands on the establishment. Why were the cutlets half cold?

Why was the tea five minutes behind time? Why did nurse pinch her sometimes in the " message "? She was loth to tell tales of a fellow-servant, but——

Then one day came the thunderclap. They told her that she was getting so much better and stronger that it would soon be time to take her to the seaside to complete the cure. Complete the cure! And then?—back to the boards again, to add more and more miles of scrubbing to her dismal count. It was wicked—the more so for their mealy-mouthed way of putting it, for she knew exactly what it meant. No doubt they had complained about her to the duchess, and she was to be turned off.

Every meal was now a conceivable last meal, every kindness a sort of mocking ministration to the inmate of a condemned cell. She had heard of that sort of thing before—buttered toast and anything else you liked to order for breakfast; and, ten minutes after, the rope round your neck.

They were uneasy on their side: something had happened to retard the cure; there was no doubt of that. The big doctor came twice in one week, the little one sometimes twice in one day. They prescribed, especially for the most alarming symptom, her frequent muttering in her sleep. It was many nights before the watcher was able to mark the sheet " rest unbroken," but it was a great relief to them when it came. The breathing was regular, the attitude one of calm and refreshing repose; it seemed a new turn of the tide.

They gave her a full extra hour next day for the morning visit. Then, in drawing up the blind to waken her, they saw by the streaming sunshine that she was dead.

They contrived to escape a coroner's inquest, with its almost inevitable verdict of " Died of the Rest Cure "; but the family solicitor advised that it might be more prudent to close the Home.

NEW OPENINGS

"Poor old lady!" said the Ratepayer with a sigh; "you see, she had nothing but her respectability, and that's a poor stock-in-trade. There's too much of it in the market: demand and supply —you know what I mean. Honesty, sobriety, attention to business, a civil tongue in your head, and all the rest of it—they're on hand at every street corner: look at the advertisements! Must have your wits right, nowadays, as well as your behaviour.

"This brings me to an idea I've often thought of speaking to you about. You see, I've got one more lad to start in the world: Don't you think we've got to find out new openings in business— new lines? There's plenty of money, but we want more ways of getting at it. In my earlier day you went into trade, or into what they call the professions, and you did pretty well. It was a living, at any rate. All that's changed now, especially in the professions.

"We want more professions—that's what I'm driving at. There are all sorts of things coming up, if you can catch on.

"What's this 'Literature,' for instance, that they talk about so much in the papers, with a

heading all to itself, just like the Money Market—
'The Book Market,' as they call it sometimes? I
believe you do a little in that way yourself. They
tell me it's a gold mine, if you can give people
what they want—prose and poetry, and all that
sort of thing. Anyway, the prose. The other, I
hear, is pretty much what it always was: my old
grandfather once gave a poet somethin' to eat—
aye, and he wanted it, too! You should have
seen the house where the poor chap was living at
the time—so I'm told. For that matter, they're
not much better off now: hardly one of 'em rated
above seventy pound, and the brokers often in at
that. Poetry! somebody's generally the worse
for it, writers or readers: it ought to be scheduled
among the dangerous trades.

" What I'm after is the business lines—writing
novels and plays and such-like. Why, Charles
Dickens—you've read his works, I'll be bound:
wonderful clever man—coined money, though he
didn't know how to take care of it. So might
Shakespeare if he had lived in our time, what with
his acting and his management, to say nothing of
writing the plays. Too many irons in the fire, to
my taste: I wonder the plays turned out so well.
As it was, you see, he was able to retire in a small
way. It wants a bit of a knack, no doubt, but I
daresay practice makes perfect in that as in most
things, especially if you keep your eyes open and
study customers' tastes.

" Well, I wish you'd tell me a little about it—
I mean as a way of boiling the pot for a young
fellow who wants to start with just two or three
servants, risin' to a man in livery as he gets on.
I had a fancy that way myself, when I was a child,
and my dad used often to wonder what was going
to become of me, but I settled down. I've quite
got over it now.

" I've been putting two and two together about
it myself, but I want you to help me out. This
is about as far as I've got : if you're going in for
literature nowadays you must be a bit of a crank,
or pretend to be. It's a sort of clowning, but of
course you must know how to clown. There's a difference between one man and another man even in
that—between a mere nobody at a fair and a Joey
Grimaldi at Drury Lane. The writing seems to be
all done by eccentrics now—people who can't keep
their hair on—you know what I mean. You've
got to say funny things and to live a funny sort
of life. I don't exactly mean a bad one, but something that looks as if it might be, for two pins.
Don't be too regular, if you can help it : people
have enough of that at their own firesides.

" We've all got to do as the others do, no
doubt, but we mustn't do it like other people—
see? You may say, why should a fellow have to
make an ass of himself just to make others take
him for a wise man ? It pays : you can't go beyond that. If you keep it up long enough the

papers will run you for a novelty, and p'raps give you a symposium all to yourself. (By-the-bye, what's the exact meaning of that word?) Then there's interviews; what you eat and drink; how you wear your hair, and such-like—small things, I daresay, but all good business. It makes you a bit of a character, and keeps your name before the public—that's the secret: you can't go wrong there.

"I've often thought that what we call literature and art is just a way of making people say 'Oh!' You *must* do that: no squeak, no sale. I had to listen to a lecture on a great German writer the other day—Prophet of Pessimism, that was the idea—and you never heard such stuff in your life. But it was funny stuff, I will say that. I couldn't get out of it—president of a sort of Mutual Improvement Society in my quarter—it's all in the play for my little game. Well, that German chap was clean off—not like poor Sam, shamming, but real bad.

"His idea, it seems, was that all the big people ought to keep all the little people down, and sit on 'em hard. It was all like that—what they call comic relief. The lecturer—funny sort of character himself—gave us a lot more of it, chapter and verse; and I took notes of bits that tickled me here and there. How will this do for a few of 'em?— 'Sin, a Jewish invention'; 'Life, something essentially immoral'; 'Remorse, an indecency:

not your sin, but your moderation crieth unto
Heaven '; ' Punishment does not purify, because
crime does not soil.' You should have heard how
they took it. ' Oh ! oh ! oh ! ' and ' Ho ! ho ! ho ! '
to follow, from first to last. One silly fellow tried
to go for the lecturer, but we soon had him out.

"The audience liked it—that's the point; and
I'm told that people pay to see it in print. It
sells; and it's literature—that's what I'm coming
to all the time.

"Now I'm going to ask you a curious question.
Can this sort of thing be taught for a premium,
and, if so, how and where? Could you put me
on to one of the fellows at the top of the tree in
this line, so that I might article my boy to him,
fair and square, to learn the trade? I don't care
what I pay in reason if I can see my way ahead.
I should look upon it as a favour, I assure you.
Business, as we generally understand it, is in a
regular slump, and we must find new openings.
Why not this one, eh? Turn it over in your mind,
and let me know.

"New openings—that's the idea. A friend of
mine who has just come back from America tells
me it's wonderful what they are doing in starting
fancy religions. They've made a perfect study of
it—just for money-making; and, by all accounts,
they're opening branches in this country. Many of
'em who used to be in patent medicines are taking
to it, and doing well. Wake up, John Bull !

" If other people can do it, why can't we? That's what I want to know. Look at that Scotsman who went out there, started a brotherhood, built a temple, and went ahead with pay! pay! pay! all along the line, and no nonsense about ' Blessed are the poor.'

" If I could write stories, do you know what I'd do? I'd write a story for business men—' Old Mr. Midas,' say, for the name. Well, he has five sons, and he's done as well as he can for four of 'em, on the old lines, but he's got the fifth on his hands, just as I might have my lad. So he sort of 'prentices the boy to a starter of new religions.

" Well, the youngster is quick at it; and, after he has got through with his master, he sets up for himself, with his father's help, and with a brand-new article of his own. At first it is slow work. All the sons come together once a year at the old man's table to compare notes, and for a long time the new apostle doesn't make much of a show. One of the brothers is a company promoter—it is before the crack—another in a wheat gamble, and so on. They are all very good friends, but the others rather look down on the one ' in religion,' and offer him presents just to help him on. That doesn't last for ever. He draws ahead bit by bit in his annual turnover, until, by George! sir, he beats the lot.

"All he wanted was time to ripen his plans;

and when the harvest comes it is a full one. He has taken up virgin soil for the settlement, sold it in lots at five hundred per cent. profit, and what with the initiation fees, the extras for the inner mysteries, the literature, and all the rest of it, he's now making money hand over hand.

" How do you like the idea? You're welcome to it, if it's of any use. It's of none to me. I know very well that there are things you may do, things you may not do, and things you mustn't be caught doing; and, at my time of life, I can't take risks. I only mention it just to show that there's always a way of getting a living, if only you know how a living is to be made."

THE CHANGELINGS

I NEVER wrote that story, but I did make some sort of a beginning with another, which, after a fashion, owed its inspiration to the Ratepayer. The following rough draft of " The Changelings " came to me in a fit of impatience with my old friend, which was more immediately due to his last communication. He was becoming rather flat to the taste, if I may put it in that way.

It must be remembered that, while I had known him but as a ratepayer, his earlier confidences had—undesignedly, I am sure, on his part —given me pictures of a more attractive personality. I say this because it is clear that his later portrait of himself as a citizen of this world, instead of as a guileless immigrant from another and a fairer one, was in his view entirely a change for the better. It was pitiful.

It was partly by way of cheering myself with a more generous conception, partly by way of escaping the Ratepayer and the annals of his maturity, that I sat down one day in a white heat and threw off this story of " The Changelings." It is one, I venture to say, which, if not exactly founded on the facts of incident, is absolutely founded on the fact of life. It remains at best but a story that was never written, but I give it for what it is worth as a fragment of improvisation that still may have its use.

The changeling-in-chief was a burglar's son, and he was substituted at birth for the infant son of a duke in a manner absolutely unknown to the parents on either side. I am not going to tell you how it was done, or why; such detail does not belong to this preliminary stage of the idea. For that matter, almost any penny dreadful taken at random will satisfy your curiosity on that point. Such matters are the very stuff of which dreams at that tariff are usually made. The motive may perhaps be a desire for vengeance on the part of a menial smarting under the sense of a real or fancied wrong; or it may be traceable to a far-reaching and subtle intrigue to divert the succession to another branch.

It really does not matter a brass farthing. The exchange of parts is all I care for now—the duchess's child spirited away from the arms of a sleeping mother at midnight, to take his place at the breast of a burglar's wife, while the poor burglar's child, suitably apparelled, is transferred as swiftly and as nefariously to the ducal mansion, to bring false comfort to the other bosom so cruelly bereaved. Both women, of course, are asleep at the time, amid suitable circumstances of squalor on the one part, and of opulent splendour on the other. I am indebted for this part of the idea to the story of Prince Camaralzaman and the Princess Badoura in " The Arabian Nights," where all the needful changes and substitutions are made while the parties most concerned are entirely unconscious of what is going on.

I must candidly confess a certain poverty, in the present instance, of convincing detail. But the reader has only to come to my assistance by taking everything as proved, as they take darkness in broad daylight on the Chinese stage. With a little co-operation of this kind in regard to other parts of the narrative, all difficulties will be effectually removed. And it must not be forgotten that, as a touch of actuality in local colour, I have placed the ducal mansion and the lodging in the slum back to back in Mayfair, as they are to be found to this day.

So the duchess awakes, still in pain, but with the rapture of motherhood conquering the pang, to clasp the burglar's child to her heart, for a first kiss, and almost without being aware of any interval between her first faint glimpse of him and the one in which all his beauty is now revealed to her delighted gaze.

A most singular circumstance must here be mentioned: a tiny arm, stretched instinctively to meet the maternal embrace, bears a well-defined strawberry márk. The duchess smiles, and the duke, who has now been summoned to the chamber, makes the inevitable allusion to the farcical incident in Box and Cox—henceforth to become one of the standing jokes of the family.

The burglar's wife meantime, while caressing the substituted infant by her side, misses the mark of this kind with which, as she had learned from an involuntary cry of the midwife concerned in the imposture, her child was born. But she is now easily persuaded by the woman that it was all her fancy, and that at any rate the mark has now wholly faded away. The medical attendant is but a confederate of the nurse, so there is no one to tell the poor mother that, in the brief interval between the two incidents, the substitution has been made.

The poor woman is too busy with other cares to give herself much concern in the matter. Her first hug of the supposed treasure, while equally intense with that of her defrauded sister in high life, has not the same character of a lengthened sweetness long drawn out. She wonders how she shall possibly manage to " rare " him (she means " rear ") until her man " gets to work again." The latter is at present at Parkhurst on a five years' " stretch " for a burglary with violence. The young mother could almost wish that she had not been brought up respectable, so that she might do a little shop-lifting or " pockets " on her own account.

She has been cruelly deceived in marriage. She was a servant in a great family in the country, and when her suitor came down as a house-painter from town and won her heart, it did not occur to her that he might be a mere scout for a gang of thieves. She never suspected it, even when the house was broken into, and cleared of a great haul of plate and jewellery.

The pair did not meet again until the affair had blown over, and she received an uncouth letter from her adorer inviting her to resume their walking out. The fact is, he had been, after a fashion, deceived in her as she in him. He had begun by using her as a dupe to be cast aside when done with, and had ended in loving her on her own account, and feeling that he could not live without her.

They were married, he still posing as a respectable man. The poor woman was gradually enlightened, but the mischief was done, and she now loved him both for himself and as the father of the child that was on its way. Before it arrived there had been a terrible scene between husband and wife in jail, in which he had made as full a confession as was consistent with his sense of loyalty to his pals. To the last she was led to believe that his share in the burglary was only the effect of a momentary aberration, and that he was to come out to resume a life of honest courses.

Perhaps he meant it when he told her so: his eye had moistened at the thought of the baby, with a tear that was really the pledge of a generous resolve. He was spared the struggle of putting it to the proof: before the time came for a second visit to him she was officially notified of his wholly unexpected death.

And now the baby had come, and the young mother, waking from the trance of agony in which she had borne her real offspring, hugged all unsuspectingly the ducal substitute to her heart, and made vows for his future.

The story now claims an interval of years. It was an interval filled, on the humble mother's side, with the most heart-rending vicissitudes of the struggle to hold body and soul together for two, and to keep both souls pure. She was more determined than ever on that, for there was the child to save. She did her best in odd jobbing, in factory work, in anything that came in her way, and went through experiences of the most sordid labour which it would be tedious and sometimes disgusting to relate.

The child was well cared for, and the health and strength that were his portion from both father and mother made him the king of his gutter when he was able to run alone. Sometimes he ran in the scantiest garments, and was probably none the worse for that. It was the life of the primitive savage in a belated survival, though the natural conditions perhaps left something to be desired. The running brooks were denied him, and the puddles were a poor exchange. The best thing was the gushing fountain of the water-cart, which washed and braced him in one operation.

He was hearty, dirty, and happy, and in all physical attributes a model of a boy. The moral conditions might have been improved. He owned no law but the law of force, and he fought steadily for his place in the sunlight with no mercy given or expected on either side. Like the rest of us, in fact, he was absolutely the creature of his surroundings, even when he occasionally swore at his mother as a protest against the excessive ardour of her embrace. He meant no harm by it: the oaths were but a part of his local vernacular, and he was really not a bad sort of fellow all round.

The burglar's son in the meantime had become an equally perfect heir apparent in every engaging attribute of body and soul. He was cheerful and good tempered, and his sincerity made him not so much incapable of a lie or of an evasion as unconscious of the need of it. Truth was in his eyes, and from them it passed spontaneously to his lips. He had never known harshness; his companions were high-bred children trained under the care of the most cultured women of their time. The world of his experience was all beauty, both to the senses and the soul. His playground on wet days was the great gallery of the ancestral home in the country, where he looked on nothing that was not an imperishable monument of perfection in the fine arts. In fair weather he exchanged this for the English or Italian gardens of the mansion, or

Q

for the charms of the almost untouched and quite unspoiled nature beyond.

In this way he caught, I will not say the trick, but the natural habit of the calm of his class, a calm bred of freedom from the baser worries, from the miseries of indigence and the meanness of the competitive struggle. It was so natural to regard all men as his brothers, for all were helpful to him, and whichever way he turned he met a smile. Everybody wished to please him, and, as a natural consequence, he wished to please everybody. In one word, it was well with the child.

He was in this respect, to compare great things with small, exactly in the same case as an animal bred for the uses of affection. It was not that the snap had been taken out of him : it had never been put in.   It is the starved and the oppressed brethren of the order that give the dog his bad name. When he is in no fear that the hand extended to stroke him may be raised to strike, he naturally welcomes its advances. .The little duke thought that fellow creatures were delightful things, no matter what their condition, and he enjoyed them as the air and the light. He had naturally the same soothing idea of life at large, for. it was so very nearly all beauty to him that its occasional lapses into ugliness only entertained him with the sense of incongruity. In this way he laughed at persons who lost their tempers, since none ever lost their tempers with him, and he knew not what it was to feel irritation, either in body or in mind.

He had no laboured choice to make of lines of least resistance, since his whole path was smooth. Like a motor-car on a good road, he was thus free from the tyranny of a set course, and able to move in any direction, according to his wish. He was still too young for wonder at the follies of the world, but he once showed intense curiosity as to the meaning of the word " pessimist," which he had encountered in the course of a reading lesson, and finally dismissed it from his mind as the synonym of a monster of fable. He had never to be warned against coarse language, since he scarcely knew of its existence. The talk that reached him was music to the ear, and his circle was as full of that and all other harmonies as a fairy round. Bad habits were out of the question, since the good ones came to him as matters of course, and he " caught " health of all kinds as others less fortunately placed catch disease. Judge how proud the duchess was of her boy.

Her husband, the duke, was denied his full share of that happiness : he was killed in the hunt-ing-field within a few months of the birth of the child that he fondly regarded as his lawful heir. It was a dreadful blow for the wife, but I pass it over as a mere incident of my story, because it has no connection with the main event. In this case, as in the other just mentioned, bereavement only strengthened the widowed mother's devotion to the infant now in her sole care.

The first suggestion of a certain finish wanting in the outlying parts of humanity came to the little heir presumptive—for so we might more properly call him—in a curious way. The duchess was a patron of a town charity, and in that capacity she gave a treat to the poor of her favourite slum. They were to drive to a lovely villa on the Thames which was a smaller country seat of the family within easy reach of town. There had at first been some talk of an excursion by train and brake to the great house in the Shires, but this was given up as impracticable. The tired mothers had to be thought of, to say nothing of the smaller fry.

The party set off in all the glory of a spring morning, three vanloads of them, the children roaring themselves hoarse in hurrahs which perhaps lacked precision of purpose, the mothers beginning to fret from sheer habit as soon as they had taken their seats, and the elder girls instinctively following their example as a sort of training for life. The sun shone on their white collars and aprons and on their parti-coloured flags: it was a pretty sight, and every 'busman made way for them with the respect due to Arcadian recollections of his own youth.

The duchess and the little duke were waiting for them on the steps of the villa, and they were soon dispersed in happy groups about the grounds.

The young heir, shaking off his attendants, ran from group to group, and took part in their sports. It was his first object lesson in the seamy side of existence. He observed some of his visitors with a pained surprise; for he could not acquit them, in his impartial mind, of being personally at fault in their frequent misadventures of dress, manners, and speech. Why were they so rough, so coarse, and even so foul-mouthed, in both kinds—with the refuse of sweetmeats and with bad language? It must be because they wished to be so, but what were you to think of people with tastes like that? For naturally he had wandered among the boys, and among these he came across two or three specimens that smote him with amazement and distress.

One little ruffian in particular, who had already appropriated a girl's hat in exchange for his own, was proceeding to trim it with blossoms which he tore red-handed, as it were, from the duchess's favourite flower bed. The little duke. gently remonstrated, and showed him how easy it would be to help himself, with permission, without injuring the roots. The urchin laid his own spoil on the ground, half abashed, half enraged at what he regarded as the other's airs of superiority, and, threatening to give him " a shove in the eye," squared up to him, and began to suit the action to the word.

A footman, who saw the sacred person of his

master in danger, ran forward just in time to avert the blow, and to counter it with a smart box on the ear. The offender roared, and his dam, recognising the cry among the hundreds then striving for mastery, made with all speed for the scene of conflict—which the duchess reached at the same time as a reinforcement for the other side. In another moment the two mothers stood face to face, each shielding the child that was dearest to her in all the world.

Naturally the voice of the crowd went up in execration of the offender, and this one, as we have seen, was the putative child of the burglar, and the rightful heir to the estate. The whole scene thus became one of the ironies of circumstance, but it is needless to say that circumstance had the joke all to itself.

The eyes of the duchess flashed inquiry and displeasure, the eyes of the other defiance and rage. Neither spoke, but, with a bitter look at her hostess and the heir presumptive, the burglar's wife gathered her brat to her bosom, and made immediate preparation for shaking the dust of the estate from her feet.

The duchess recovered herself in a moment, and was about to make investigations when the false heir, true to his gentle upbringing, cut the whole matter short by springing forward to take the other's hand, and to tender his own humblest excuses if he had been in any way to blame. No less true to the manners of his slum, the true heir responded with an ill-conditioned offer to " tike " his infant host " with one 'and," in quite another fashion, whenever he liked. The slum mother chid him for his rudeness and burst into tears, while the crowd hailed this prospect of peace with a cheer. The other child, however, was quietly removed to another part of the grounds, the duchess dismissing him to the care of a governess, with a kiss, as the undoubted winner of the honours of the day.

So the pair grew up, the duke's son into a coster, as the result of a brave effort on the part of his supposed mother to provide him with an honest calling. She had pondered many things in her heart, among them the incident of the abortive birthmark which had so mysteriously disappeared; and this determined his vocation. Though a confessed delusion, it was still an omen, and her boy should sell fruit and vegetables in the streets. Heredity had not led him into burglary, for she had taken care that he should never learn that art, nor have any knowledge of its existence, and had kept him free from all its associations by the most persistent efforts of devotion. But she could not save him from vulgarity, since this was the very air he breathed. In other respects he was equally the product of his surroundings, and every Sunday morning, in fine weather, he was a Socialist.

The little duke " in being " meanwhile continued to advance in all the graces of his part. The public school and the university did their best for him, travel gave him the finishing touch; he was beyond every temptation to excess, since the most refined pleasures in life were always within his reach. He had that almost innate moderation which, in the matter of raspberry tarts, is said to characterise the children of persons in the confectionery trade. He had but to ask to have, and therefore it cost him no effort to refrain. He was a keen, though not a fanatical sportsman, for moderation was the note of his nature, and he instinctively felt that over-indulgence in any one pleasure would spoil his appetite for the rest.

He took his place in the House of Lords in due course, and in his first session had the honour of moving the Address in answer to the Speech from the Throne. He acquitted himself with the perfect ease of one who has been acting in a representative capacity all his life. He had never spoken at less than his best, and the slight difference in the circumstances could not weaken the wholesome tyranny of habit.

If there was any tendency to excess in his exquisitely balanced nature it was in his devotion to the duchess. She at least had reason to suspect that this feeling made him unwilling to think of marriage. She knew that he had fixed his affections on the daughter of the clergyman who held the chaplaincy of the household—his one departure from the conventions of his order. But she was also aware that, while true to the girl of his choice, he was unwilling to take any step that might force the consent of one whom he still chivalrously regarded as the head of his house. The matter was left in abeyance; and, meanwhile, the preparations were already advanced for the somewhat long-deferred celebration of his coming of age.

These had just been completed in every detail when mother and son, if we may call them so, suddenly made the discovery of the dreadful secret of his birth.

It came as a thunderclap, and its immediate cause was the death-bed confession of one of the nurses who had been engaged in the fraud. I must decline once more to go into further particulars on the point, since the elaboration of them belongs to quite another stage of my story. Moreover, I always grudge the time wasted on these details, and in actual execution would willingly send them "out," like the washing of a well-appointed household. The soul of a tale of this kind is in its idea. I know I shall be told that it is quite the other way: to this I have but one answer — fiddle-de-dee! respectfully but firmly, fiddle-de-dee!

The hints I have already given must suffice. It is enough to say that the other persons engaged in the wretched business were a doctor in poor

practice, and a messenger, now in the workhouse,
who, at the time of the almost simultaneous birth
of the two children, carried a wicker basket to the
house in the slum with orders to wait for a return
load. The rest is silence and mystery, and so is the
question whether these humble agents of infamy
were but the tools of others in a higher sphere.

Fate had timed the disclosure for the opening
day of the rejoicings, and for the moment when
the hitherto undisputed heir to the title, after a
busy day among the revellers, was going to snatch
a moment's rest before the torchlight procession
that was to bring the pageant to a close. He
and the duchess had just entered the great hall
when they were urgently summoned to the library.
Here they found the costermonger, and two persons of more civilised appearance who turned out
to be his solicitors, and who carried a formidable
array of papers. With many apologies, and some
credit claimed for themselves for their delicacy in
not making their errand public at this stage, they
begged the duke's attention to a matter of the
greatest importance, and at the same time asked
him to summon his own solicitor, whom they had
recognised among the company in the grounds.

They then proceeded to give a brief outline of
their claim to the title and estates, and to vouch-
safe a confidential sight of certain papers which in
their judgment proved their case beyond all possibility of dispute. They wound up by presenting

as " our client the duke " the dejected individual who had hitherto stood silent in the background, and who wore a new suit of ill-fitting broadcloth evidently ready-made.

The duke in possession had maintained his composure up to this point, but when they supplemented their evidence with the mention of the strawberry mark, he turned pale and grasped the back of a chair. The duchess showed signs of the most violent agitation from first to last, and once or twice was with difficulty prevented from ordering the dismal deputation from the premises. Her distress culminated in a fainting fit when the costermonger, in response to a sign from one of his advisers, stepped forward with a cry of: " What cheer, mamma! won't you kiss your boy? " and a gesture which plainly signified his intention of clasping her in a filial embrace. This was too much, and she had to be carried out of the room.

After a slight upset between the men of law, the interview ended in an appointment for the following day at the same time and place. The family solicitor was at first strongly opposed to this course, but his client, now the only level-headed person in the company, put an end to the discussion with a tone and gesture of authority, and bowed his strange visitors out. He would not even consent to have himself excused from the festivities on the plea of ill-health, and he carried through the mockery of rejoicing to its bitter end of the torch-light procession.

The extraordinary claimant and his advisers, who had meantime been lodged at the village inn, returned to the castle next morning, and, after several visits of the same kind, completed, still in confidence, the outline of their case. The family solicitor resisted to the last, and vigorously pooh-poohed the importance of the suggestion that the substituted child and false heir palmed off on the duchess must be still bearing the birthmark, while the true heir, who had been palmed off on the burglar's wife in exchange, had really never borne it in his life.

He was proceeding to argue that this was but negative evidence at the best, when his client, who had shown some signs of impatience, said to the costermonger :

"You have a question to put to me, I feel sure. Do me the favour to put it at once."

"Thank you kindly," replied the claimant, "and 'umbly beggin' your pardon, but have you such a thing as a strawberry mark on your left arm?"

"Yes," returned the other unhesitatingly, and laughing for the hundredth time at the time-honoured formula of the family joke.

"Then excuse me, my lord," said the claimant, "I must be the long lost hair."

The other laughed again, and who could have

helped it with the logic and the lingo so beautifully matched? Then, suddenly baring his arm, he called on his rival to do the same.

The result was that, for a moment, the two claimants accidentally stood once more in the fighting attitude which the meaner one at least had assumed in the quarrel in the grounds.

This, however, was but a coincidence; the main thing was that the false heir bore the tell-tale mark. He now made no secret of his conviction that there was some show of a case, and insisted on being made a party to a friendly action for a settlement.

This action, to make an end of a tedious tale, after being carried from one court to another, was finally settled in the costermonger's favour by the highest tribunal in the realm. The evidence as to the birthmark was, of course, but the smallest part of the case: it was a great trial with an extreme complexity of issues, and it had far-reaching echoes throughout the whole English-speaking world. Needless to say, however, that the popular literature of the time was affected by a kind of sympathetic rash on the subject of birthmarks which raged for months in both hemispheres.

The rest is soon told. The unhappy duchess never accepted the evidence on which the claim had been established, and consequently never saw her real son again. It would have killed her to admit that, in any conceivable circumstance, such a mother could have brought forth such a child. She declared that the only birthmarks she could be induced to recognise were those of character, and that she should consider herself for ever bound by a thousand ties of affection to the splendid specimen of cultured manhood she had reared as her own.

She and her favourite left soon after for Italy. They were not alone, for she had fully withdrawn her opposition to the marriage of the one who must now be called her adopted son with the woman of his choice. The villagers took a most affectionate leave of them, and all declared that they had never encountered such a true duke as the false one in the whole course of their lives.

The false duke was perhaps the only person entirely satisfied with the result of the affair in all its bearings. Left to the full enjoyment of the society of the two beings who were nearest to his heart, he was without a care—except such as arose when those about him extolled the chivalry which had prompted him to declare his full adhesion to the evidence against his own claim. How, he would ask, could he possibly have acted otherwise, considering by whom he had been brought up, and he would seal the declaration by pressing a kiss on the duchess's brow. He was, no doubt, a little too much of a gentleman, if that were possible, but it was a pardonable fault.

He paid several visits to his poor coster mother

before leaving England, and he offered to stand by her to the last. He did full justice to her excellent qualities, though he was spared all knowledge of the fact that, had he never been taken from her side, her motherly devotion would still have saved him from growing up as a cracker of cribs. The good woman, however, repelled his advances, as the duchess had repelled those of her own son. She could not unlearn where once she had learned to love; and to the real duke's credit he was equally unwilling to make any experiment of the kind on his own behalf. He settled her in suitable circumstances in an ornate villa at Upper Tooting, and continued to visit her at intervals to the close of her life.

His Grace, as we must now call him, was less successful as a duke than as a costermonger. He had usually risen to his opportunities, as we have seen, in the readiness with which he became an honest man when his foster mother relieved him of the cruel necessity of following her husband's trade; but he lacked suitable training for his new part, and this was not to be acquired at his time of life. With better fortune he would certainly have made an excellent nobleman, for he was richly endowed with the attributes due to the in-breeding of his long and pure descent. He had come of the best stocks for at least five hundred years, and it is notorious that these are also the worst in regard to the transmission of the stronger qualities of mind and heart. There must be a healthy infusion, somewhere, of the strength of the soil, even if it should take the form of an occasional barmaid.

The duke had thus most of the qualities, positive and negative, for his position—and, I may say, without malice, one of its most precious defects, in being by nature a nobody in particular. All he wanted was manners and customs to set them off. He was pre-eminently simple in his tastes; but it was a real misfortune that his simplicity took the form of scattered aspirates, peas with a knife, and " 'arf and 'arf " out of a pewter pot.

He hovered, as it were, between two conditions; and he could not forbear from ordering a set of " pearlies," and contemplating them on birthdays in the seclusion of his dressing-room. He was, of course, debarred from every kind of fashionable sport, and his skittle parties were a poor compensation, since both he and the old friends he invited from town agreed, in their secret hearts, in calling them " cold." What else could they have been? The skittles were set up on the beautiful bowling green instead of in the back yard of the public-house, and his attempt to transfer the game to that quarter only led to the immediate resignation of his butler.

He found some slight compensation in bird fancying and in an occasional dog-fight; and his ratting sports in the beautifully upholstered pit which he had constructed on the site of the historic flower-bed in the duchess's garden yielded a languid glow of satisfaction from time to time. As he said truly enough to the gardener's man, his only confidant in the household, it is easy enough to be a duke if you have learned the trade, but you can't do it self-taught.

For this reason he took care to make the schools on the estate the very best in the land. No one could tell, he said, what heir to what other peerage might languish in the obscurity of village life, and it would be a thousand pities to deny any possible candidate the means of taking his rightful place in society without a sense of embarrassment. " It ain't 'ow you're born, it's 'ow you're eddicated," he observed in his first distribution of prizes. I give the remark as it fell from his lips—I need hardly say with no design of bringing ridicule on one of the worthiest of men.

LITTLE GREAT PEOPLE

I HAD thought to have done with his Grace here, but it is impossible, for he flowered into good works towards the close of his life. The end, however, came all too soon : he did not long enjoy his honours. In a few years he was gathered to his fathers in the family vault, and, so far as can be known, they received him without a shudder. He had unusually long obituary notices in the newspapers; the costers followed him to the grave; and a donkey, bearing a pair of Blücher boots reversed across the saddle, walked in the procession.

His will was a disappointment to some of his humble friends, and a surprise to everybody. It was found that he had left a large sum to found a vast philanthropic institution for the benefit of the idle rich. His scheme included a domestic mission for the conversion of this much-neglected class. There were to be preachers to call them publicly to repentance, good men and women to carry the pure word of social salvation to them in their homes, and even rescue bands to catch them, as it were, on the hop of frivolity in their favourite haunts.

In the preamble to this curious document, the testator expressed his firm conviction that those of his noble order were the most unhappy people in the world. This, he went on to say, was no fancy on his part; he knew it by his having tried to live up to their ideals.

He was thinking of a time when, weary of his old associates and their pleasures, he had felt it his duty to adopt the social code of his station. It was no easy matter, for, as we know, his education in things of this sort had been grossly neglected. He was, however, equal to the occasion; and, in the belief that it is never too late to mend, he secured the services of a venerable lady who lived by taking persons in his predicament in hand. He placed himself unreservedly in her care, and she undertook to teach him how to behave, as though he were but a child of the larger growth. It was dear, but the case was desperate, and he had a long purse.

She began, more like a doctor than a governess, by a process of purification. His old costermonger friends were sent to the right about, and he was put on a low diet of decent company in the shape of the local curate and a couple of impecunious squires who had never before seen the inside of the Hall.

Meanwhile she conversed with him for his h's; and, without entirely curing him of his peculiarities in the treatment of them, gradually induced him to temper injustice with mercy. He tried, as he phrased it, to "blow" into them in the right place, and to play them more gently at least in the wrong. She dined with him three times a week, and by coughing every time he threatened to use his knife as a ladle, induced him to give the other implement a chance. She bought his ties, on commission, and even showed him how to put them on. Moreover, she led him gently to the happy mean between the sullen ferocity which was his first idea of repose, and the practice of slapping people on the back when he felt at ease with his company.

The next stage was his first dinner party, composed of the faithful parson and squires, with a few who were not so fully in the secret.

It went off quite fairly, though unfortunately the duke's tutor seemed far from well. She coughed nearly all the time. In the excitement of the new ordeal, his Grace reverted to primitive habits, and drew his blade on his food in a manner that seemed to threaten the destruction of the whole party. He was also a little below the dignity of his part in calling for "a little drop of unsweetened" when the liqueurs went round. But most of his friends understood, and all took it in good part. They felt that in a person of his rank such faults were but virtues on the seamy side. Intolerable in one of less importance, in him they seemed but the charm of a simplicity that became his state.

And one day when they shared his hospitality with another duke it was generally agreed that, in regard to the grand manner, there was hardly a pin to choose between the pair. Each in his way did exactly as he liked, as though afraid of nothing under the sun. Even when the host turned his back on his guests, by inadvertence, as they entered the room, they gave him the benefit of the doubt in trying to believe that he had done it by design. In being formless, in fact, he was a mould of form, and his admirers fondly revived their stories of the good old sort who, when they were not in their robes, were usually to be found in their shirt-sleeves.

Finally his mentor ventured on the great experiment of giving him a season in town. His reputation had preceded him; he was asked everywhere; and at every turn he blundered into fame. The women got out of his way, for his path was marked by the ruin of their skirts, but they laughed as they fled. All were ready to believe the best of him; and his " blowed if I know " in intellectual difficulties was taken as a turn for repartee. In short, though it was a bold experiment, he came well out of it by the simple expedient of being true to himself.

For him it was an extraordinary experience. He had had many a season in town from the kerbstone; this was his first from the carriage drive. There is nothing like it in the whole world for the suggestion of something too good—or, according to the point of view, too bad, to last. Thousands poured in every day from all parts of the planet, with half of its wealth in their pockets burning to get itself spent. How he had once envied, hated, and denounced from the kerb! How good it all now seemed from the drive! But this sense of fruition was not to last, for the earlier feelings still claimed their rights. He had acquired among his new accomplishments the art of reading the *Morning Post* as it is read by the scholars of fashion; and its serried ranks of engagements, arrangements, and what not for the day and night awed and at last frightened him outright. It seemed like the daily report of some force of nature on a path of ruin, a blizzard in full blow, a herd on the stampede—and it bore the same suggestion of an utter want of ruth. It might be all very well while you were out of reach, but what if you stood in its way?

Even his power of making the money fly with the best of them was disquieting. Could he be sure that the revel would last his time? He was grateful to the policeman who held up the traffic for his carriage to pass. Balls, parties, dinners, races, and all the rest of it—when might not the thunderbolt fall? The old envy and hatred of others were now a new misgiving for himself, for he could still read the faces of thousands whose share in it was not so much as " the price of a pint." ·

The last stage of his apprenticeship was a visit
to a mansion where he was to see how things were
managed in an establishment of the first class.
He went over it like a child, under the guidance
of his lady help, wondering, fingering, threatening the pictures and the statuary with the point
of his umbrella. At first he could hardly pass
the threshold for fear, when giant footmen swung
the doors open to admit him, while others stood
in line as though to forbid him the path. He
recovered his spirits when he came to some of the
ancestral portraits. He called them " cures," as
they faced him in corselet or in gown, and wondered how they were ever able to take one another
seriously.

He insisted on seeing everything from cellar
to garret, and he made remarks, not altogether
without illumination, on such things as he was
able to understand. But one thing utterly puzzled
him—a suite of offices on the third floor that
formed the secretarial department of the great
house. Here, in one capacious room lined with
shelves, they kept the list of all their acquaintance, and essayed the difficult feat of knowing the
whole human race within the boundaries of
fashion. It might easily have been mistaken for
a secret service chamber of some bureau of
police. Everybody that was anybody was pigeon-
holed or entered in the books. Busy typewriters
seemed to tick off the seconds from the cradle to

the grave, cards were filled in by the basketful, envelopes addressed in sheaves, the very stamps were passed through a machine.

In an inner room sat the chief, another of the lady helps of fashion. This high officer, from whom there was no appeal but to the head of the house, knew the exact hierarchical standing of all the worldlets that make the world. She decided such knotty points as the transfer of sinners who had been found out from the list of the sheep to the list of the goats, or the reversal of the process for the benefit of those who had lived it down. She elevated or degraded authors as they fared in the current demands at the libraries and the verdicts of the reviews, placed the company at dinner parties according to their eternal value in rank or in real estate, or their temporary value in vogue. Her hair was as white as snow.

The intricacies of the whole business, the ins and the outs of it, were extraordinary. There were secret memoranda in whole volumes, with confidential entries against particular names. Some were blacklisted for offences against the law, others for lack of royal notice or of social form. To the simple-minded visitor, it seemed like a wanton anticipation of the rigours of a last assize.

What did it all mean? The duke's mentor soon enlightened him. As a great noble and leader of society he had to know everybody worth knowing, and to know of a good many not worth it; and this was how it was done.

This, moreover, was how the duke would have to do it. The poor man took up whole bundles of cards of invitation, and let them fall through his fingers like withered leaves. Every one of them, he was made to understand, signified an acquaintance who might never be a friend; and often an acquaintance beyond all possibility of recognition. If, like a second Samaritan, he found one of them fainting by the way, he might have to say : " Excuse me, but I haven't the honour." And yet they, or hundreds like them, were coming to him next week, and he would at least have to pretend that he knew them all.

" Not me ! "—and he countermanded his own revel on the spot, dismissed his lady help—not without the promise of a liberal solace—rushed to a low public-house in his own neighbourhood, and came home " elevated "—for the first time since his elevation.

It was all over, and he went back to resume his skittles, his bird fancying, his beer, and the extremely select parties of his old coster friends— never to try to be a great nobleman again.

The rest of his all too short life was devoted to the philanthropic attempt to convert the idle rich to a sense of the error of their ways. He was convinced, he said, though he said it in his own way, that if they could only be brought to take a saner view of existence the poor would easily manage for themselves. The true social question was for Belgravia, not for Seven Dials.

With him, for he was a man of action, this conviction was no sooner formed than he set to work on it. He was lucky enough to find a second Charles Booth to give shape to his ideas, and both were soon engaged on a colossal work entitled, " Fashion and Foolery in London," which promised to throw the " Life and Labour " into the shade.

It was in the main a vast tabulation of all the misery due to the abuses of wealth and luxury in modern Babylon. Its charts of the areas of idleness in that square mile of fashion which holds all that we regard as most precious in England were marvels of completeness. The chapters on Wealth and Crowding Out—Birth Rate and Death Rate of the Peerage—Marriage and Morality in Mayfair —Sundays, Holidays, Amusements, and Week-Ends—Betting at Tattersalls and in the Ring— were heartrending in their disclosures as to the condition of the unfortunate few of our fellow creatures cursed with the birthmark of the silver spoon.

The noble author was especially severe on flats in the chapter headed, " The Slums of the Rich." Most of them, he said, were not to be compared with the dwellings of this sort provided for the poor, with their minute statutory provision for light and air, their ample courtyards, and especially their entire freedom from black holes. In the more stylish structures every inch of space had been utilised to the point of suffocation, and the innermost courts were often but vertical tubes, with dárkness visible at the bottom, and hardly a breath of air anywhere. As he justly observed : once let an infectious disease find sanctuary in such a labyrinth, and it might defy pursuit.

The root idea of the whole work was that we could hope for no salvation for this particular class of the submerged until we learned to tell the truth about them without fear or favour, and to keep our pity to ourselves.

It is pleasing to be able to say by way of postscript that this good man's closing years were brightened by the society of a wife after his own heart—a young washerwoman who had often bought goods at his barrow in earlier and better times, and who made him one of the happiest of men.

CREATURES OF THE WILD

I FOUND them in a quite civilised region flying the British flag, a place of industry and manufactures, with tall ships going to and fro, and the music of distant hammer on metal all day long. They were but half wild: civilisation had caught up with them at last, and set them to work. The mission settlement stood by them in the trial.

It lay on a tiny island, itself an effect of nature not unassisted by art. This had begun apparently as a small peninsula jutting out into a river, and had finally achieved independence of the mainland by means of a canal. I saw it under misty skies, streaked but now and then during the time of my stay with the sun. But the suavity of it was perfect. All around, the yellow water, the wharves, the shipping, and the sluggish shipmen in the haven enjoying the pleasure of equilibrium between spells of ocean storm. Nothing so restful as a ship—when it does not happen to be the most fidgety thing in the world—and nothing more restful than a sailor. He relaxes every muscle, and he knows that the fewer buttons the more rest. His brew of tea is perfection, his herring is done to a turn. The ship enjoys itself as much as he does, and its timbers cease to creak their protest against the worries of life.   Cleaning-up time, when men revert to the severities of the Puritanism that is in all of us, is for by and by.

The mission house had been a seat of local administration in earlier times. The hall below us was now used for pictorial lectures suited to the level of the native mind, and for an occasional dance. Above was a sort of common room for the ladies in residence, simply and therefore perfectly furnished, with bedrooms and sitting-rooms beyond. It was the repose of the cloister without its solitude and its chill—the wherewithal and no more : a few prints and photographs on the distempered walls, a few knick-knacks on the tables, pretty but useful still. The plain yet perhaps costly homespun of the sisterhood—if sisterhood it was to be called— was in the same style. It was the Quaker note, in the putting away of foolishness, but still with something left to keep touch with the world. They wore no uniform either of luxury or of renunciation : in fact, the whole impression may be best put in this way—both manner and attire—" without frills."

Many were women of fortune and position, who had left a life of ease for the refreshment of this change to first principles.   It was no formal divorce from pomps and vanities, only a periodical escape from them, by way of retreat. They had to take a holiday at short intervals, as a servant might be compelled by a wise mistress to take her

Sunday out. With these precautions they were kept up to the highest condition of efficiency. Their table was served without any affectation of the pulse and beans that make for self-consciousness in matters of this sort.

Presently it was time for a visit to the factories, under the guidance of one of the band. We went through clean streets, well laid out as to breadth and straightness, with abundance of air in the unimpeded breezes from the river, and of light in the rows of huts all innocent of a second floor. Then came a great shed, where native women were employed; and here a change. It was a rope factory, new style, filled with costly machinery wholly superseding the old-fashioned rope-walk. I yearned for the superseded thing as I had known it in the rural suburbs, with its trees not altogether innocent of birds—a conceivable haunt of the peripatetic school. The machinery required care; and as it was shut in from the weather, the touch of nature was entirely out of the question.

It was at rest now for the dinner hour, but how it must have roared and fumed when it began work again! And how the dust from the hemp, now enjoying the siesta in its own way, must have filled the whole place under the lash of the troubled air!

The women crowded round us, leaving their pannikins of food, and our conductor doled out an offering to the tribe. It was " sweetstuff " for this occasion. They stretched out eager hands for it, though their ages ranged from seventeen to thirty and forty years. All were infants, in their boisterous laughter and shrill delight, in the very mildness that might yield to its opposite at a moment's notice. One dreaded that possible second state. The twenty pairs of strong arms, tearing as one, would soon make fragments of the strongest man. The twinkling eyes could be terrible, if the sparks in them happened to be of the wrong sort.

It was a strange impression for one used to womanhood of the ordinary pattern. Here were creatures in petticoats who might thrash you at need, and make you howl for mercy in sheer physical pain. What a gulf between them and the gentle ministrant who ruled them with her smile! What ages of all the cultures of mind and heart from the starting point of the primitive brute! Their rags of labour added to the terror of their aspect; with their wild hair, long since shaken out of its coils, they seemed of the Gorgon breed. Such shapes, such faces no doubt formed the gauntlet at the gate of the Abbaye, in that awful jail delivery of old. One felt thankful for the policeman in reserve, for the sister at hand, with her bag of lollipops.

Thence to the two mission churches, both barns in their structural scheme, but barns of perfect symmetry and proportion, and what is a Tuscan temple more? In one the walls were of plaster, with a toned wash highly effective in its suggestion of absolute purity; in the other, of red brick, inside and out. But, with this as a background, there were many prints of the Arundel Society, with their ineffable beauty of expression and right down sincerity of holiness in every laboured line. On these, with their frequent and beautiful variations of the Mother and Child, one might imagine the little wild people gazing at the hour of service as at something beyond and above themselves.

The altar, with its ever burning lights and highly ornate symbolism, was another thing to hush and tame such beholders with a sense of mystery not of this world. The adjoining church-house was, in part, a place of recreation, and it had its stage for lectures and for plays, possibly of the miracle order. Everything, here as elsewhere, and especially in the church, was as comely as the gifts of the rich, the pocket money of the priest, and the pence of the worshippers could make it.

The next and the last stage was the parson's home. This, and the like of it, may yet save our civilisation in the last resort. Here was a man of the high breeding of his cloth, probably one reared from the cradle in great comfort, with his sister, roughing it in three rooms and a kitchen on the top floor of a "model," at a rental of about six shillings a week. The humble lodging was not for show, but for use; yet it was quite beautiful in its harmony with the ideal of apostolic poverty. And with that, the parson might save something from his stipend for the adornment of his church and for works of charity. The rooms were almost ridiculously small. The man's was a kind of mechanical puzzle : when the bed was on duty the study was off, for sheer want of elbow room ; when the study came on, the bed had to be turned up to the ceiling. The lady's room, I believe, had precisely the same character of a cupboard giving itself airs. The remaining apartment—drawing-room, dining-room, sitting-room by turns—offered you a choice of contact with the furniture or with the other inmate.

The priest was all cheerfulness and simplicity— a great boy in nature as in build, Goliath of Gath in a bandbox. His simplicity was particularly charming. He congratulated himself on our having come on the very day they had laid down their new hearthrug—perhaps just to clear his own mind of the cant of asceticism. Then he went on to talk of his plans for his natives. They needed a cheap eating-house, where they might get clean, well-cooked food at just as little as would pay expenses. This would give them something warm inside for their breakfasts in the winter darkness, and something comforting at all times.

And now it is time to drop the fable, and to be more precise as to place and circumstances. The suggestion throughout—artful or not, according to

s.

the measure of its success—has been remoteness, as of a thing going on in some wild, outlandish part of the world. But in truth my island is but the Isle of Dogs, at the bend of the Thames by Greenwich Reach, as my natives are persons of our own racial flesh and blood. The shipping, too, is only the shipping of the India Docks. And the beauty of it all—for beauty there is—is still English in its softening and blending atmosphere of purple haze.

As we mounted the roof of the model—flat, for use as a drying ground—we were told of distances touched in summer with the glory of spires and of verdure-clad hills. And we saw masts, quite as imposing in their way as forests, with a site where Frobisher had built, and where Raleigh had perhaps smoked as he watched the galleons that were one day to bear him to his fatal quest. "Here and nowhere else is America," says Goethe's hero to a fellow creature pining for the opportunities of a distant scene. And here, in the Isle of Dogs, a region that is no more than an unsavoury name to most of us, may be found in full the satisfactions of the gentle life. The charm of it for the people of the mission is evidently that it is a land of the romance of fine deeds. They are cheerful as sportsmen on a hunting morning. No doubt they rise every day with the sense that there is grand game afoot—poverty to be relieved, sickness soothed, savagery tamed. This last above all.

On the sordidness of the region, if you choose to look for it as they have to look, I have forborne to touch. For one reason, because it is but the thrice-told tale of all the cities of the wide world in those parts in which so many dwell. For another, because, revolting as it is as an economic condition, it has still much saving beauty of a certain down-rightness to the eye. The slum is a thousand things that are hateful, but it is rarely quite ugly. Its life is so intensely varied, its races are drawn from so many parts of the earth, and each brings a note.

And then again I wish to preserve the impression that those who are called upon to better it are called fine in a certain sense, to the highest joys. But for all this, of course, one could have said more of the little failings of a social scheme that offers women and girls, at the end of their week of ten and a half hours a day of hard and often disgusting labour, the sum of eight shillings and ninepence all told. One day, perhaps, some plan of distribution that begins with the worker and the inalienable decencies, and takes the profit earner only last of all, may oust this from its pride of place.

Still, matters being as they are, one can hardly wonder that some despairing wretches, so paid, forgetting what fine qualities may be cultivated on a little oatmeal, squander their whole pittance on the witch's sabbath of a " Saturday drunk."

In this state, I believe, the women stand up to one another like men, in the inevitable fight, and punish with the knuckle instead of with the claw.

I dared not touch on another reflection with the cleric, but it may have its place. What a colossal difficulty to square the Christian teaching with the facts of life for those to whom it is offered here! That teaching is a sort of fair play in the highest between man and man. But how harmonise it with enterprises that give these workers their eight-an'-nine, and their employers, no doubt, the usual percentage of profitable investment? It must be a real difficulty where the workers have half the aptitude of the Zulu for question and answer.

Pity the poor priests so handicapped! Most of them have no sense of their burden, but preach a cheerful optimism, as though the problem were the simplest in the world. The minority feel the pressure, but worry through with their load. As a matter of fact, they are rarely called upon to put a penitent in his place. Dumb acquiescence is the rule—with the faint hope of being one day able to serve one's fellow creatures in the same way. The harshest things, however, are said for the sufferers rather than by them at the Sunday preaching of revolt in all its varieties at Mile End Waste. The risk is that it needs but a strong wind to blow them to every hovel. The trouble for the Church is that most of the clergy don't want to preach social justice, for lack of the sense of it, and the others don't dare. So, much of the suffering of the time which is purely economic in origin and nature, clerical ministrations fail to touch.

The coster duke knew what he was about—the real battle of the East End is to be fought in the West.

LITTLE PEOPLE IN REVOLT

IF ever these people get out of hand! That was how it struck me as I left the island. Personal fears, now that I was on the safe side of the water, gave way to a lively concern for the security of things in general. What of a revolt—not of the rope-makers merely, but of all the nobodies, all the failures—all the Little People.

Might not one picture them as rising at length, in their might of collective feebleness, with a determination to have it out with their masters, the clever fellows? For these, with all their cleverness, are still but the garrison of a conquered world. If the others timed their rising by an electric tick running round the planet, where would that garrison be? It would need no determination to do or die on the part of the entire horde; a determination of the rear ranks to make the front ones push on would be quite enough. Sheep sometimes conquer dogs in this way, and red ants men.

For the clever fellows, as at present organised, are a provocation and a bore, in spite of their platitudes about their beneficent mission. In earlier ages such upstarts were accepted as fate; to-day they are questioned everywhere as super-

fluity. It is a new time, with its new varieties of
the itch of revolt, and it no longer takes a knock
on the head for the cure.

The modern protest is against the enormous
value the clever fellows set on their labours. They
do " lay it on so " in their bills for social service.
They have contrived to make everything an extra,
even their self-denial, until the unfortunate traveller
on life's highway curses the day when he first put
up at their inn of The Golden Fleece all ignorant
of the cryptic meaning of its sign.

After all, why should the mere want of cleverness entail such heavy penalties? Or, to put it
in another way, why should the Little People suffer
so severely for the fault of a shortage of brains?
That commodity was never nearer the top of the
revel than it is to-day, yet how galling to poor
stupidity to have no share in the fun. It might
be less so if our rude earthly Providence reserved
all its favours for the competent. As it is, your
dead hand of the right sort can sustain any amount
of incompetence in perpetuity on the fat of the
land.

The strong democratic reactions of the time have
this at the root of them, however they may try to
conceal it with the verbiage of the mealy mouth.
Their " right to live " is really a claim for the right
to play up Old Gooseberry with the best.

When the commissioners of the first French
Republic were sent to the provinces to make

inventory of the forfeited estates, they at once began to play the fool on their own account. They held high revel in the halls of the banished aristocracy; their suppers were a terror; their dances would have put Dionysus to shame. The virtuous citizens who had not been invited asked for an explanation. "It is our turn now," was all they got for their pains.

This is the cry of all the democracies—new style. Figo for all our make-believe on both sides! We don't pretend to be better than our betters; our humble plea is that a good time is a good thing.

The danger is that we may have this, or something like it, upon us at any moment. Talent has no new sense of its responsibilities, virtue has taken no new lease of life; the only thing that has happened is the rather sudden demise of the patience of the Have-nots, and with it the equally sinister new birth of appetite as the law of life.

It is land hunger, and the rest of it, only in one of its aspects; it is pleasure hunger below that. Never have we all been so eager for our interlude of high jinks on the way to the crematorium. Our choice of this now fashionable mode of exit is significant; it precludes identification, and may still enable some of us to cheat the Recording Angel of his due. The more prudent have their ashes scattered to the wind. Stole away! The churches, lay and clerical, are equally at a loss for the valid word, and the whole Positivist section coo in vain their doctrine of the supremacy of the wise. The clever fellow is the enemy.

The peril in question is, of course, only an insurrection of ideas. That is why it may prove so irresistible : it is like a rising of the tide. Insurrections of the other sort have an unfortunate habit of getting beaten, if only for lack of ammunition. Ideas can be manufactured by any man, and stored by all; and every stump of every tree of knowledge in our public places is their magazine.

So, prudence would suggest some modification of our public policy, at least in the way of inviting our poor relation more often to the board. He chafes at our luck, and passionately claims some recognition of the relationship. We have to minister to his appetite, not indeed so freely as we minister to our own, without any condition as to merit of any kind, but at least with some decent pretence of being glad to give him his fill. It need be no question of our love for him : our love for ourselves will do.

We have still our prophet in Nietzsche, with his cry of " Down with the weak." But imagine a new movement in philosophic literature to the tune of " Down with the strong " ! At any moment a sling and a stone from the ranks of the Little People might do the business of the pessimist in vogue. The slinger could make out just as good a case for them as their arch-enemy has made for his " laughing lions " gobbling up all weaker things

in their scorn. It would be paradox against paradox at the worst; and, at this game, one cannot be
too bold. For years the prophet has had the field
all to himself, and deserved it by the audacity of
his claim. He found mankind still writing in its
copybooks that the strong ought to spend themselves in the service of the unfit. He quietly proposed to send all the unfit into the lethal chamber,
and he at once led the literature of an empty day.

It would never do to have the Little People pleading humbly for notice and consideration. There
should be no plea at all, but an imperious demand,
with a " Be quick about it ! " for the rider. Who
made them weak? And, weak as they are, nine
times nine of them might yield a man strong
enough to thrash the tallest of their foes. " Let
us in, or we'll spoil your universe ! " What a
cry !

A LITTLE SAINT

She did not grumble at her lot, though she was but a poor little lodging-house keeper by the sea. Yet, could she have known it, there was no living in any true sense of the word by the doll's-house to which her exertions were confined. There were but eight rooms in all, and she and her children lived in the kitchens to give the upper floors their full chance as bread-winners. But what else was she to do? A larger house would have involved capital or the risk of debt. The capital was not in her pocket, and the debt not in her nature.

Like most dolls'-houses it was neatness itself. Perfection was the word from the back yard to the entry that would hardly take a full-sized trunk. It shone under her labours: the stair-rods flashed high light almost without the aid of the sun. No temple could have been cleaner—and it was a temple in itself, the temple of 'Ome.

She and her two daughters were priestesses, both of the rite and of the service of purification. They were at it all day long, scouring, dusting, and setting to rights. As the single gentleman in the parlours, I found traces of their care whenever I came in, even from posting a letter. The

crumpled sheet, which had missed the waste-paper
basket in the fine frenzy of an aim intent on higher
things, lay in the basket on my return.

She faced her lot fairly, with all its privations—
her lot of widowhood, with the two girls to bring
up, and with the huge drop in income due to the
loss of her husband's salary of thirty shillings a
week as a clerk in a store.

The three together not only did all the housework—they made all the clothing, with the aid of
patterns supplied by her religious paper, *The Ban-
ner and the Shield*. There was but a single exception : mantles were beyond her reach. One was
bought yearly and passed on. The elder girl began
with it, and wore it till it fitted the younger; finally
the patient mother had her turn, and cleaned and
pressed it for the meeting-house, where it was only
two seasons behind time. I must not forget to say
that, with all this, they made the bread, and reared
the fowls that supplied the eggs—for the single
gentlemen. The household was thus self-sufficing
as any family of the Middle Ages, in being bakers,
tailors, dressmakers, dyers all in one. It was also
its own carpenter and its own upholsterer. Every
curtain was made, and every nail driven in by the
same hands that did the rest—the tacks with the
old hammer scarred by long service, the larger
varieties with the flat iron kept as a force in reserve.
In one respect it was as most houses of its class :
At every point of the compass you were confronted

with a decorative Scripture text bearing counsel for the holy war. The hall exhorted to faith, the sitting-room to hope, the first landing to charity.

The mother evidently rejoiced in the conflict; the girls, I thought, sometimes showed the dejection of the conscript serving against his will. They seemed to have seen nothing but furniture polish, done nothing but scrub and mend, and to be under the oppression of a moral atmosphere overcharged with care. Yet they professed a high sense of opportunity, though perhaps more as a matter of belief than of evidence.

When the single gentleman was of the right sort they were allowed to take him for walks in the neighbourhood. This, however, was really a part of the housework, for cheerful society was guaranteed in the advertisement. They said but " Yes " or " No " to him at first, until, thawing under the fire of his questions, they began to show some concern in human affairs at large, as these had come within their ken. Their interest, however, was still confined to the doings of the lodgers. One of these, another single gentleman, obviously a lunatic, had been sent down for the fresh air. To their apprehension he was only a strange gentleman, but as such he had made some faint impression on their minds. It appeared that, although fifty years of age, he rarely went anywhere without holding on to his mother's gown. On one occasion he was entrusted to the two girls,

and he acquitted himself fairly well until he met
cows. Then he bolted, and left his companions
to shift for themselves.

They admitted that he was rather funny, but
their experience was so bounded that they had no
idea of what was really the matter with him.

Two girls of their acquaintance had their
brother for keeper whenever . they walked out.
When he was not available they stayed at home,
sometimes for days together. One of them, however, managed to get an invitation to London, and
was said to have lapsed into dancing parties and
going to the play. Fired by her success, the other
followed her to town, and found work there. Both
wrote to say they were happy, and wouldn't come
back for all the world. The captives of the 'ome
often mentioned them, by desire, in their prayers.
You see, as they explained, the danger was that
men might speak to you if you were out by yourself.

I asked if this difficulty might not be met by a
less heroic sacrifice. They made no reply.

Their talk kept the promise of social entertainment, as advertised, to the spirit, if not to the
letter. If not exactly cheerful, it was decidedly
interesting. Here, at any rate, were the Little
People in almost their full perfection of insignifi-
cance. And there were more and richer confidences to come.

It was a hushed Sabbath afternoon, at the hour

of the siesta, between early dinner and tea. The little mother, smartened up for evening chapel, came into my sitting-room—uninvited and, but for her knock, unannounced. It was a first visit, and a compliment altogether beyond the stipulation of the bond.

The conversation began with the weather, but soon passed to topics suited to the day, and finally settled on the subject of the visitor's religious beliefs. Then, gradually, and with no more deliberation on her part, I feel sure, than expectation on mine, she laid bare the innermost soul of one of the Little People to my astonished gaze.

For now I learned that the sure and the sustaining hope of my little landlady was fixed on an almost immediate beginning of the millennium here below, with an uncontested reign of its Saints over the whole earth for its full term of a thousand years !

"At any moment ? " I gasped, for, I hardly know why, I was frightened to think it was so near. " ' As between to-day and to-morrow,' I think you said that."

"As between to-day and to-morrow," she answered firmly, " for aught we know."

"And all the powers of the earth overturned, and the—the—your friends put in their places for ten times one hundred years ? "

She nodded.

" The same Saints all the time ? "

" The very same."

" Yourself among the number, I trust," said I, with an air that would have been fatuous as gallantry, though it was perhaps excusable as an attempt to gain breath. The suddenness of it all was too much for me. This, then, was what had upheld my landlady in all the troubles of life, this was the secret of her interest in a tiresome perspective of single gentlemen of which I was the vanishing point.

" Why not? " said she.

"As absolute rulers of the whole earth, our own country included ? "

" Beyond a doubt."

" Ruling the land," I went on—" Local Government Board, and all that sort of thing ? " It was rather hard on her, I admit, but I could not help trying to get it right, as a sort of otherwise incredible statement in confession which she might be required to sign.

" Oh, as to that we don't know, and we don't care, so long as it is governed properly. It wants governing, I fancy; it doesn't get much of that now—three murders last week ! "

"And, of course, you'll expect to be called Secretaries of State, and such like, if you do the work ? "

" We shall be called the Saints," she said sharply. " That's good enough for us."

The thought of her exercising administrative

functions in this exalted sphere transcended all ordinary effects of its kind. For a space I was perfectly mute.

" You've no misgivings about your being able to take all our little affairs in hand at short notice in Europe, Asia, Africa, and America ? "

" We are the Saints : all knowledge will come to us, and all power. I suppose you haven't got as far as Revelations. We shall be ready, no fear, whenever the signal comes, and it is about due now. All the signs point to it; the papers is just brimful of them, if they only knew, poor things ! if they only knew ! You should hear our preacher; and p'raps you might like to see this (holding up her weekly paper). That's what I'm livin' for : you don't suppose it's lodgers ! "

She corrected herself with an air of apology. " Not but what they're all very well to live by."

" What a mighty change it will be ! "

" All the proud ones of the earth abased," she said with fire, " all the wise confounded, all the rulers put to shame—leastways if they are not Saints."

" What is a Saint exactly ? "

" Don't you know ?—them as hold the faith."

" There are so many faiths."

" There's only one accordin' to the Book, an' there's only one place here and there that's got it right."

" Rather hard on the others."

" Wilful blindness."

" What faith is it, I wonder ? "

" Oh, I can't go into that.   You can come with me to-night, if you like, an' you'll soon see."

" How shall we know when the thousand years begin ? "

" You'll know fast enough, sir," she said softly and half in reverie.   Then, as the vision of signs and wonders took full possession of her soul, the eyes glowed, the face shone as in the light of a whole system of suns.

" But the Saints who have gone to their rest— are they to have no part in it ? "

" They'll rise," she said decisively, as though disposing of a childish question with a single touch.

" In their bodies as they lived ? "

" In their living bodies, free from all taint of flesh—bodies that will last a thousand years and a thousand thousand after that."

" It's what you may call glorified flesh," she added after a pause, yet as familiarly as though she was talking of some process of the toilette.   This was the note all through—a homely, an almost sordid precision of detail, and the highest rhapsodies ; the seer of Patmos and the little landlady turn and turn about.

" You can't understand these things, sir, but it ain't your fault, it's the fault of them as brought you up."

"And the living Saints—will they be transformed in the same way?"

"'In a moment, in the twinklin' of an eye'—that's what the real meanin' of the text is. No more whitlers then," she added with a little laugh, and looking down at one of her fingers in its stall. "But there, p'raps you'll see for yourself : you've been a good lodger to me, sir, I will say that."

"It's glorified flesh," she added, after a pause, "incorruptible; and everybody'll have it as deserves. Them as don't 'll live and die just as they do now, till the thousand years is over, and all rise for the great day."

"Will there be any chance for them?"

She looked uneasy. "Well, there may be, I daresay, if they'll let theirselves be ruled. But, of course, they can't expect——"

"Even the kings and princes and rulers of the earth, the great as well as the little?"

"They must do's they're told," she persisted; "can't say more than that. The Saints'll be all right, that's all I know; and when they've done their work, they'll go straight up to their everlasting 'ome, without death."

"After the thousand years?"

"After the thousand years."

For the rest, my account of the really stupendous utterance of the little landlady must fade off into loose notes. She is beyond my power of adequate presentation—in the mingled pettiness of her person and surroundings and the majesty of her claims.

Her heaven, I found, was a quite hierarchical scheme, though with new values by way of compensation for the shortcomings of earth. The Saints were a sort of natural aristocracy, kept out of their own by usurpations, but sure to come back to it. She was not an Englishwoman for nothing, and she expected to find her kings, lords, and commons in every state of being. Equality no more had a place in her vision than liberty, and even fraternity was but a sort of accident. People were made to be ruled, but, of course, only by the right sort.

Her ideal was hardly less materialistic in its nature than it was aristocratic. Heaven, she informed me, was a place of actual mansions made with hands, though with hands that were divine. The just would be housed there according to their degrees, not of wealth or station, as in this world, but of holiness. The one great qualification was faith.

And this was still strangely associated in her mind with leanings, purely mundane in their nature, towards an aristocracy of caste. John the Baptist, she assured me, was really quite what might be called a gentleman by origin. Her paper or her preacher—I forget which—had recently discovered that, and she had been one of the first to hear of it. He was descended from Aaron, and so belonged to an excellent family.

She was a Dissenter, but she seemed to have no hard and fast objection to any particular form of belief consistent with the one that lay nearest to her heart. When she lived in another part of the district she used to attend a Presbyterian church, but that was too far away now. So she went to a Baptist church at present, because, you see, it was only the penny fare.

She sometimes went to the Quaker meetings. The Quakers were very nice people : their preachings were open to women. It was a good idea— why should not a woman have a right to say her say ?

She took a great interest in faith healing, though she knew nothing about it as an organised cult. She knew of it only through her own experience. As a visitor to the sick, she had lately cured a cobbler by this process. He was dying of something, bronchitis or consumption, no one exactly knew what. His lungs were " furred, black as soot," with the impurities of his trade. The doctors had given him up. She asked him if he had faith, and he said he thought he had. She said thinkin' wouldn't do; he must say " Yes " or " No." She prayed with him, and he said " Yes." The next day he was perfectly well.

She left me presently, and went to pack my traps, for I was leaving that night. When I got

home I found a present in one of the pockets. It
was a tract containing a brief exposition of the
perfect way.

It is my happiness to be able to take my leave
of the Little People with this extraordinary and
most sympathetic figure. Here is an absolute, and
beside that, in its perfect flower, the merely relative
can never have a chance.

By the sheer good luck of the order of my
fancies, I began my book with this idea. For
those childish intuitions of the good and the true
with which most of us most certainly start are
absolutes too. The old friend who has aecom-
panied me so long on the way through its pages
himself began in that manner. It was subsequently his fate to show what the world sometimes
makes of us before it has done its deadly work—
not by any means all villains, but so often anything but heroes—Ratepayers, in one word.

My landlady had evidently kept faith with herself from first to last. She saw this whole scene
of life as nothing but a glorious opportunity of
being true to those earliest beliefs that come spontaneously into the healthy soul. For her, existence was a divinely appointed struggle; and
courage, endurance, and all the other virtues of
the battlefield a divinely appointed means of
victory.

We have heard of the religion of a physician;
here is the religion of a little landlady; and one

is just as important as the other. I shall ever think of her as a sort of queen of the Little People. It may be that every one of them, in his secret heart, dreams of being somebody, somewhere, someday, if not of a whole millennium of mastery over the powers of this world.

THE END

PRINTED BY
CASSELL & COMPANY, LIMITED, LA BELLE SAUVAGE,
LUDGATE HILL, LONDON, E.C.

Lightning Source UK Ltd.
Milton Keynes UK
UKHW020638241218
334505UK00007B/364/P